CHRISTOPHER WILLIAM BRADSHAW ISHERWOOD was born in England in 1904, briefly attended Cambridge, and briefly studied medicine. His first novels, *All the Conspirators* (1928) and *The Memorial* (1932), have been praised for their literary brilliance, but it is for his "Berlin novels," *Mr. Norris Changes Trains* (1935) and *Goodbye to Berlin* (1939), the basis for the highly acclaimed musical *Cabaret*, that he is most famous. During the same years, he collaborated with W. H. Auden on a number of plays: *The Dog Beneath the Skin* (1935), *The Ascent of F6* (1937), and *On the Frontier* (1938).

Mr. Isherwood left Europe in 1939 and came to California where he wrote Hollywood screenplays and his later novels—*Prater Violet* (1945), *The World in the Evening* (1954), *Down There on a Visit* (1962), *A Single Man* (1964), and *A Meeting by the River* (1967). He became an American citizen in 1946 and settled in Santa Monica where his friendship with Aldous Huxley inspired the religious pursuits that have become an important part of his life. He is today a student of Vedanta and has written extensively on various aspects of Hindu philosophy. In recent years he has been active as a guest lecturer and visiting professor at distinguished universities, and has become an increasingly active supporter of gay liberation.

Other Avon books by
Christopher Isherwood

PRATER VIOLET

CHRISTOPHER ISHERWOOD

 A BARD BOOK/PUBLISHED BY AVON BOOKS

AVON BOOKS
A division of
The Hearst Corporation
959 Eighth Avenue
New York, New York 10019

First Bard Printing, January, 1978

BARD TRADEMARK REG. U.S. PAT. OFF. AND IN
OTHER COUNTRIES, MARCA REGISTRADA, HECHO EN
U.S.A.

Printed in the U.S.A.

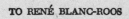

TO RENÉ BLANC-ROOS

"MR. ISHERWOOD?"

"Speaking."

"Mr. Christopher Isherwood?"

"That's me."

"You know, we've been trying to contact you ever since yesterday afternoon." The voice at the other end of the wire was a bit reproachful.

"I was out."

"You were out?" (Not altogether convinced.)

"Yes."

"Oh . . . I see . . ." (A pause, to consider this. Then, suddenly suspicious.) "That's funny, though . . . Your number was always engaged. All the time."

"Who are you?" I asked, my tone getting an edge on it.

"Imperial Bulldog."

"I beg your pardon?"

"Imperial Bulldog Pictures. I'm speaking for Mr. Chatsworth. . . . By the way, were you in Blackpool any time during 1930?"

"There must be some mistake . . ." I got ready to hang up on him. "I've never been to Blackpool in my life."

"Splendid!" The voice uttered a brisk little business laugh. "Then you never saw a show called *Prater Violet?*"

"Never. But what's that got to do with . . . ?"

"It folded up after three nights. But Mr. Chatsworth likes the music, and he thinks we can use most of the lyrics. . . . Your agent says you know all about Vienna."

"Vienna? I was only there once. For a week."

"Only a week?" The voice became quite peevish. "But that's impossible, surely? We were given to understand you'd *lived* there."

"He must have meant Berlin."

"Oh, Berlin? Well, that's pretty much the same kind of set-up, isn't it? Mr. Chatsworth wanted someone with the Continental touch. I understand you speak German? That'll come in handy. We're getting Friedrich Bergmann over from Vienna, to direct."

"Oh."

"Friedrich Bergmann, you know."

"Never heard of him."

"That's funny. He's worked in Berlin a lot, too. Weren't you in pictures, over there?"

"I've never been in pictures anywhere."

"You haven't?" For a moment, the voice was audibly dismayed. Then it brightened. "Oh, well . . . It'll be all the same to Mr. Chatsworth, I imagine. He often uses writers who haven't had any experience. If I were you, I wouldn't worry . . ."

"Look here," I interrupted, "what is it that makes you think I have the very slightest interest in taking this job at all?"

"Oh . . . Well, you see, Mr. Isherwood, I'm afraid that's not my department. . . ." The voice began to speak very rapidly and to grow fainter. "No doubt Mr. Katz will be talking things over with your agent. I'm sure we'll be able to come to some arrangement. I'll keep in touch with you. Good-bye . . ."

"I say, wait a minute. . . ."

He was off the line. I jiggled the phone for a moment, stupidly, with vague indignation. Then I picked up the directory, found Imperial Bulldog's number, dialed the first letter, stopped. I walked across to the dining-room door. My mother and my younger brother, Richard, were still sitting at breakfast. I stood

9

just inside the doorway and lit a cigarette, not looking at them, very casual.

"Was that Stephen?" my mother asked. She generally knew when I needed a cue line.

"No." I blew out a lot of smoke, frowning at the mantelpiece clock. "Only some movie people."

"Movie people!" Richard put down his cup with a clatter. "Oh, Christopher! How exciting!"

This made me frown harder.

After a suitable pause, my mother asked, with extreme tact, "Did they want you to write something?"

"Apparently," I drawled, almost too bored to speak.

"Oh, Christopher, how thrilling that sounds! What's the film going to be about? Or mustn't you tell us?"

"I didn't ask."

"Oh, I see. . . . When are you going to start?"

"I'm not. I turned it down."

"You turned it down? Oh . . . What a pity!"

"Well, practically . . ."

"Why? Didn't they offer you enough money?"

"We didn't talk about money," I told Richard, with a slight suggestion of reproof.

"No, of course you wouldn't. Your agent does all that, doesn't he? He'll know how to squeeze the last drop out of them. How much shall you ask for?"

"I've told you once. I refused to do it."

There was another pause. Then my mother said, in her most carefully conversational manner, "Really, the films nowadays seem to get stupider and stupider. No wonder they can't persuade any good writers to come and work for them, no matter what they offer."

I didn't answer. I felt my frown relax a little.

"I expect they'll be calling you again in a few minutes," said Richard, hopefully.

"Why on earth should they?"

"Well, they must want you awfully badly, or they wouldn't have rung up so early in the morning. Besides, movie people never take 'no' for an answer, do they?"

"I dare say they're trying the next one on their list already." I yawned, rather unconvincingly. "Ah, well, I suppose I'd better go and wrestle with chapter eleven."

"I do admire the way you take everything so calmly," Richard said, with that utter lack of sarcasm which sometimes makes his remarks sound like lines from Sophocles. "If it was me, I know I'd be so excited I wouldn't be able to write a word all day."

I mumbled, "See you later," yawned again, stretched myself, and began a turn toward the door, which was checked by my own unwillingness, leaving me facing the sideboard. I started to fiddle with the key of the spoon drawer, locking, unlocking, locking. Then I blew my nose.

"Have another cup of tea before you go?" my mother asked, after watching this performance with a faint smile.

"Oh, do, Christopher! It's still scalding hot."

Without answering, I sat down in my chair at the table. The morning paper still lay where I had let it fall, half an hour ago, crumpled and limp, as if bled of its news. Germany's withdrawal from the League was still the favorite topic. An expert predicted a preventive war against Hitler some time next year, when the Maginot Line would be impregnable. Goebbels told the German people that their vote on November the twelfth would be either Yes or Yes. Governor Ruby Laffoon of Kentucky had given a colonel's commission to Mae West.

"Cousin Edith's dentist," said my mother, as she passed me the teacup, "seems to be quite convinced Hitler's going to invade Austria soon."

"Oh, indeed?" I took a big sip of tea and sat back, feeling suddenly in a very good humor. "Well, no doubt the *dental* profession has sources of information denied to the rest of us. But I must say, in my ignorance, I entirely fail to see how..."

I was off. My mother poured fresh cups of tea for Richard and herself. They exchanged milk and sugar with smiling pantomime and settled back comfortably in their chairs, like people in a restaurant when the orchestra strikes up a tune which everybody knows by heart.

Within ten minutes, I had set up and knocked down every argument the dentist could possibly have been expected to produce, and many that he couldn't. I used a lot of my favorite words: Gauleiter, solidarity, démarche, dialectic, Gleichschaltung, infiltration, Anschluss, realism, tranche, cadre. Then, after pausing to light another cigarette and get my breath, I started to sketch, none too briefly, the history of National Socialism since the Munich Putsch.

The telephone rang.

"What a bore!" said Richard, politely. "That

stupid thing always interrupts just when you're telling us something interesting. Don't let's answer it. They'll soon get tired. . . . "

I had jumped up, nearly knocking over my chair, and was out in the hall already, grabbing for the instrument.

"Hullo . . ." I gasped.

There was no answer. But I could hear that the receiver was off at the other end—distant voices, seemingly in a violent argument, with a background of wireless music.

"Hullo?" I repeated.

The voices moved away a little.

"Hullo!" I yelled.

Perhaps they heard me. The sounds of talking and music were suddenly cut right out, as though a hand had covered the mouthpiece.

"To hell with you all," I told them.

The mouthpiece was uncovered long enough for me to hear a man's voice, with a thick, growling foreign accent, say, "It's all too idiotic for words."

"Hullo!" I yelled. "Hullo! Hullo! Hullo! Hullo! Hullo!"

"Wait," said the foreign voice, very curt, as if speaking to a nagging child.

"I bloody well won't wait!" I shouted at him.

And this sounded so silly that I started to laugh.

The hand came off the mouthpiece again, releasing a rush of talk and music which sounded as though it had been dammed up during the interval, it was so loud.

"Hullo," said the foreign voice, rapidly and impatiently. "Hullo, hullo!"

"Hullo?"

"Hullo? Here Dr. Bergmann."

"Good morning, Dr. Bergmann."

"Yes? Good morning. Hullo? Hullo, I would like to speak to Mr. Isherwood, please, at once."

"Speaking."

"Mr. Kreestoffer Ischervood . . ." Dr. Bergmann said this with great care and emphasis. He must have been reading the name from a notebook.

"Here I am."

"*Ja, ja* . . ." Bergmann was obviously nearing the end of his patience. "I wish to speak to Mr. Isherwood personally. Please bring him."

"I'm Christopher Isherwood," I said, in German. "It was me talking to you all the time."

"Ah—*you* are Mr. Isherwood! Marvelous! Why did you not say so at once? And you speak my language? Bravo! *Endlich ein vernu-*

15

enftiger Mensch! You cannot imagine how I am glad to hear your voice! Tell me, my dear friend, can you come to me immediately?"

I turned cautious at once. "You mean, to-day?"

"I mean now, as immediately as possible, this instant."

"I'm awfully busy this morning . . ." I began, hesitantly. But Dr. Bergmann cut me short with a sigh which was nearer to a loud, long groan.

"It's too stupid. Terrible. I give up."

"I think I could manage this afternoon, per-haps. . . ."

Bergmann disregarded this completely. "Hope-less," he muttered to himself. "All alone in this damned idiotic city. Nobody understands a single word. Terrible. Nothing to do."

"Couldn't you," I suggested, "come here?"

"No, no. Nothing to do. Never mind. It's all too difficult. *Scheusslich.*"

There was a pause of extreme tension. I sucked my lip. I thought of chapter eleven. I felt myself weakening. Oh, damn the man!

At length, I asked unwillingly, "Where are you?"

I heard him turn to someone, and growl belligerently, "Where am I?" There was an answer I couldn't catch. Then Bergmann's growl, "Don't understand a word. You tell him."

A new voice reassuringly Cockney:

"Hullo, sir. This is Cowan's Hotel, in Bishopsgate. We're just across from the station. You can't miss it."

"Thanks," I said. "I'll be right along. Good-b——"

I heard Bergmann's hasty, "Moment! Moment!" After what sounded like a brief but furious struggle, he got possession of the instrument and emitted a deep, snorting breath. "Tell me, my friend, when will you be here?"

"Oh, in about an hour."

"An *hour*? That is very long. How will you come?"

"By Underground."

"Would it not be better to take a taxi?"

"No, it wouldn't," I answered firmly, as I mentally reckoned up the cost of a fare from Kensington to Liverpool Street Station: "No better."

"Why would it not be better?"

"It would be just as slow as the Underground. All the traffic, you know."

"Ah, the traffic. Terrible." A deep, deep

17

snort, as of a dying whale about to sink to the bottom of the ocean forever.

"Don't worry," I told him cheerfully. I felt quite kindly toward him, now that I had won my point about the taxi. "I'll be with you very soon."

Bergmann groaned faintly. I knew that he didn't believe me.

"Good-bye, my friend."

"*Auf Wiedersehen* . . . No, I can't say that, can I? I haven't seen you yet."

But he had hung up on me already.

"Was that the movie people again?" Richard asked, as I looked into the dining room.

"No. Well, yes, in a way. Tell you everything later. I've got to rush. Oh, and Mummy, I *might* be a little late for lunch. . . ."

Cowan's Hotel was *not* just across from the station. No place ever is, when they tell you that. I arrived in a bad temper, having been twice misdirected and once nearly knocked down by a bus. Also, I was out of breath. Despite my resolve to take Bergmann calmly, I had run all the way from the Underground.

It was quite a small place. The porter was standing at the door, as I came panting up. Evidently he'd been on the lookout for me.

18

"It's Mr. Usherwood, isn't it? The Doctor'll be glad to see you. He's been having a lot of vexation. Arrived a day before he was expected. Some mistake. No one to meet him at the boat. Trouble with his passport. Trouble with the Customs. Lost a suitcase. A regular mix-up. It happens that way, sometimes."

"Where is he now? Upstairs?"

"No, sir. Just popped out for some cigarettes. Didn't seem to fancy what we had. You get to like those continental kinds, I suppose, if you're used to them. They're milder."

"All right. I'll wait."

"If you'll excuse me, you'd better go after him. You know what foreign gentlemen are, being strange to the city. They'll lose themselves in the middle of Trafalgar Square. Not that I won't say we wouldn't be the same, in their place. I'm sure I don't know what's become of him. He's been gone above twenty minutes already."

"Which way?"

"Round the corner, to your left. Three doors down. You'll be sure to catch him."

"What does he look like?"

My question seemed to amuse the porter. "Oh, you'll know him all right when you see him, sir. You couldn't mistake him in a million."

The girl at the little tobacconist's was equally chatty. There was no need for me to try to describe Dr. Bergmann. His visit had made a great impression.

"Quite a character, isn't he?" she giggled. "Asked me what I thought about, being here all day long. I don't have much time to think, I told him. . . . Then we got to talking about dreams."

Bergmann had told her of a doctor, somewhere abroad, who said that your dreams don't mean what you think they mean. He had seemed to regard this as a great scientific discovery, which had amused the girl and made her feel somewhat superior, because she'd always known that. She had a book at home which used to belong to her aunt. It was called *The Queen of Sheba's Dream Dictionary,* and it had been written long before this foreign doctor was born.

"It's ever so interesting. Suppose you dream of sausages—that's a quarrel. Unless you're eating them. Then it's love, or good health, the same as sneezing and mushrooms. The other night, I dreamed I was taking off my stockings and, sure enough, the very next morning, my brother sent me a postal order for five and six. Of course, they don't always come true like that. Not at once . . ."

Here I managed to interrupt, and ask her if she knew where Bergmann had gone.

He had wanted some magazine or other, she told me. So she'd sent him over to Mitchell's. It was down at the other end of the street. I couldn't miss it.

"And you'd better take him his cigarettes," she added. "He left them lying here on the counter."

Mitchell's, also, remembered the foreign gentleman, but less favorably than the girl at the tobacconist's. There seemed to have been a bit of an argument. Bergmann had asked for *The New World-Stage,* and had become quite indignant when the boy naturally supposed it was a theatrical magazine, and had offered him *The Stage* or *The Era* instead. "Hopeless. Nothing to do," I could imagine him groaning. At length, he had condescended to explain that *The New World-Stage* was about politics, and in German. The boy had advised him to try the bookstall inside the station.

It was at this point that I lost my head. The whole business was degenerating into a manhunt, and I could only run, like a bloodhound, from clue to clue. It wasn't until I had arrived, gasping, in front of the bookstall that I realized how silly I'd been. The bookstall attendants were much to busy to have noticed anybody with a foreign accent; there had probably been several, anyway, within the past half hour. I glanced wildly around, accosted two likely looking strangers, who regarded me with insulted suspicion, and then hurried back to the hotel.

Again, the porter was waiting for me.

"Bad luck, sir." His manner was that of a sympathetic spectator toward the last man in an obstacle race.

"What do you mean? Isn't he here yet?"

"Come and gone again. Wasn't a minute after you left. 'Where is he?' he asks, same as you. Then the phone rings. It was a gentleman from the studio. We'd been trying to get him all morning. Wanted the Doctor to come out there, right away, as quick as he could. I said you'd be back, but he wouldn't wait. He's like that, sir—all impatience. So I put him in a taxi."

"Didn't he leave any message?"

"Yes, sir. You was to meet them for lunch, at the Café Royal. One o'clock sharp."

"Well, I'm damned."

I went into the lobby, sat down in a chair

and wiped my forehead. That settled it. Who in hell did they think they were? Well, this would be a lesson to me. One thing was certain: they wouldn't hear from me again. Not if they came to the house and sat on the doorstep all day long.

I found them in the Grill Room.

I was ten minutes late, a little concession to my injured vanity. The headwaiter knew Mr. Chatsworth and pointed him out to me. I paused to get a first impression before approaching their table.

A gray bushy head, with its back to me, confronted a big pink moon-face, thin, sleek fair hair, heavy tortoise-shell glasses. The gray head was thrust forward intently. The pink face lolled back, wide open to all the world.

"Between you and me," it was saying, "there's just one thing the matter with them. They've got no *savoir vivre*."

The pale round eyes, magnified by their lenses, moved largely over the room, included me without surprise: "It's Mr. Isherwood, isn't it? Very glad you could come. I don't think you two know each other?"

He didn't rise. But Bergmann jerked to his feet with startling suddenness, like Punch in a show. "A tragic Punch," I said to myself. I couldn't help smiling as we shook hands, because our introduction seemed so superfluous. There are meetings which are like recognitions —this was one of them. Of course we knew each other. The name, the voice, the features were inessential. I knew that face. It was the face of a political situation, an epoch. The face of Central Europe.

Bergmann, I am sure, was aware of what I was thinking. "How do you do, *sir?*" He gave the last word a slight, ironic emphasis. We stood there, for a moment, looking at each other.

"Sit down," Mr. Chatsworth told us, good-humoredly.

He raised his voice. "*Garçon, la carte pour monsieur!*" Several people looked around. "You'd better have the Tournedos Chasseur," he added.

I chose Sole Bonne Femme, which I don't like, because it was the first thing I saw, and because I was determined to show Chatsworth that I had a will of my own. He had already ordered champagne. "Never drink anything else before sunset." There was a little place in Soho, he informed us, where he kept his own claret. "Picked up six dozen at an auction last week. I bet my butler I'd find him something better than we had in the cellar. The blighter's so damned superior, but he had to admit I was right. Made him pay up, too."

Bergmann grunted faintly. He had transferred his attention to Chatsworth, now, and was watching him with an intensity which would have reduced most people to embarrassed silence within thirty seconds. Having eaten up his meat with a sort of frantic nervous impatience, he was smoking. Chatsworth ate leisurely, but with great decision, pausing after each mouthful to make a new pronouncement. Bergmann's strong, hairy, ringless hand rested on the table. He held his cigarette like an accusing forefinger, pointed straight at Chatsworth's heart. His head was magnificent, and massive as sculptured granite. The head of a Roman emperor, with dark old Asiatic eyes. His stiff drab suit didn't fit him. His shirt collar was too tight. His tie was askew and clumsily knotted. Out of the corner of my eye, I studied the big firm chin, the grim compressed line of the mouth, the harsh furrows cutting down from the imperious nose, the bushy black hair in the nostrils. The face was the face of an emperor, but the eyes were the dark mocking eyes of his slave—the slave who ironically obeyed, watched, humored and judged the master who could never understand him; the slave upon whom the master depended utterly for his amusement, for his instruction, for the sanction of his power; the slave who wrote the fables of beasts and men.

From wine, Chatsworth had passed, by a natural sequence of ideas, to the Riviera. Did Bergmann know Monte Carlo? Bergmann grunted negatively. "I don't mind telling you," said Chatsworth, "that Monte's my spiritual home. Never cared much about Cannes. Monte's got a *je ne sais quoi*, something all its own. I make a point of getting down there for ten days every winter. Doesn't matter how busy I am. I just pull up stakes and go. I look at it this way; it's an investment. If I didn't have my time at Monte, I just couldn't stand this bloody London fog and drizzle. I'd come down with the flu, or something. Be in bed for a month. I'm bloody well doing the studio a favor; that's what I tell them. *Garçon!*"

Pausing to order Crêpes Suzette, without consulting either of us, Chatsworth went on to explain that he wasn't a gambler, really. "Have to do enough gambling in the motion-picture business, anyway. Roulette's a damn silly game. Only fit for suckers and old women. I like chemmy, though. Lost a couple of thousand last year. My wife prefers bridge. I tell her that's her bloody insularity."

I wondered if Bergmann's English was equal to understanding all this. His expression was getting more and more enigmatic. Even Chatsworth seemed to be aware of it. He was becoming a little unsure of his audience. He tried another opening, which began by congratulating the headwaiter on the Crêpes Suzette. "Give Alphonse my compliments, and tell him he's excelled himself." The headwaiter, who evidently knew just how to handle Chatsworth, bowed deeply. "For you, monsieur, we take a leetle beet extra trouble. We know you are connoisseur. You can appreciate."

Chatsworth fairly beamed. "My wife tells me I'm a bloody Red. Can't help it. It just makes me sick, the way most people treat servants. No consideration. Especially chauffeurs. You'd think they weren't human beings. Some of these damned snobs'll work a man to death. Get him up at all hours. He daren't call his soul his own. I can't afford it, but I keep three: two for day and the other fellow for the night. My wife's always after me to sack one of them. 'Either we have three,' I tell her, 'or you drive yourself.' And she'll never do that. All women are bloody bad drivers. But at least she admits it."

Coffee was served, and Chatsworth produced a formidable red morocco-leather case of beautiful workmanship, as big as a pocket Testament, which contained his cigars. They cost five and sixpence each, he informed us. I refused, but Bergmann took one, lighting it with his grimmest frown. "Once you've got a taste for them, you'll never smoke anything else," Chatsworth warned him, and added graciously, "I'll send you a box tomorrow."

The cigar somehow completed Chatsworth. As he puffed it, he seemed to grow larger than life-size. His pale eyes shone with a prophetic light.

"For years, I've had one great ambition. You'll laugh at me. Everybody does. They say I'm crazy. But I don't care." He paused. Then announced solemnly, "Tosca. With Garbo."

Bergmann turned, and gave me a rapid, enigmatic glance. Then he exhaled, with such force that Chatsworth's cigar smoke was blown back around his head. Chatsworth looked pleased. Evidently this was the right kind of reaction.

"Without music, of course. I'd do it absolutely straight." He paused again, apparently waiting for our protest. There was none.

"It's one of the greatest stories in the world. People don't realize that. Christ, it's magnificent."

Another impressive pause.

"And do you know who I want to write it?" Chatsworth's tone prepared us for the biggest shock of all.

Silence.

"Somerset Maugham."

Utter silence, broken only by Bergmann's breathing.

Chatsworth sat back, with the air of a man who makes his ultimatum. "If I can't get Maugham, I won't do it at all."

"Have you asked him?" I wanted to inquire, but the question sounded unworthy of the occasion. I met Chatsworth's solemn eye, and forced a weak, nervous smile.

However, the smile seemed to please Chatsworth. He interpreted it in his own way, and unexpectedly beamed back at me.

"I bet I know what Isherwood's thinking," he told Bergmann. "He's right, too, blast him. I quite admit it. I'm a bloody intellectual snob."

Bergmann suddenly looked up at me. At last, I said to myself, he is going to speak. The black

eyes sparkled, the lips curved to the form of a
word, the hands sketched the outline of a gesture. Then I heard Chatsworth say, "Hullo,
Sandy."

I turned, and there, standing beside the table, incredibly, was Ashmeade. An Ashmeade
nearly ten years older, but wonderfully little
changed; still handsome, auburn-haired and
graceful; still dressed with casual under-
graduate elegance in sports coat, silk pullover
and flannel bags. "Sandy's our story editor,"
Chatsworth was telling Bergmann. "Obstinate
as a mule. He'd rewrite Shakespeare, if he
didn't like the script."

Ashmeade smiled his smooth, pussycat smile.
"Hullo, Isherwood," he said softly, in an
amused voice.

Our eyes met. "What the hell are you doing
here?" I wanted to ask him. I was really quite
shocked. Ashmeade, the poet. Ashmeade, the
star of the Marlowe Society. Obviously, he was
aware of what I was thinking. His light golden
eyes smilingly refused to admit anything, to
exchange any conspiratorial signal.

"You two know each other?" Chatsworth
asked.

"We were at Cambridge together," I said

briefly, not taking my eyes from Ashmeade's, challenging him.

"Cambridge, eh?" Chatsworth was obviously impressed. I could feel that my stock had risen several points. "Well, you two will have a lot to talk about."

I looked squarely at Ashmeade, daring him to contradict this. Ashmeade simply smiled, from behind his decorative mask.

"Time to be getting back to the studio," Chatsworth announced, rising and stretching himself. "Dr. Bergmann's coming along with us, Sandy. Have that Rosemary Lee picture run for him, will you? What the hell's it called?"

"*Moon over Monaco,*" said Ashmeade, as one says *Hamlet,* casually, without quotation marks.

Bergmann stood up with a deep, tragic grunt.

"It's a nasty bit of work," Chatsworth told him cheerfully, "but you'll get an idea what she's like."

We all moved toward the door. Bergmann looked very short and massive, marching between Chatsworth's comfortable bulk and Ashmeade's willowy tallness. I followed, feeling excluded and slightly sulky.

Chatsworth waved the attendant aside with

a lordly gesture and himself helped Bergmann
into his overcoat. It was like dressing up a
Roman statue. Bergmann's hat was a joke in
the worst taste. Much too small, it perched
absurdly on his bushy gray curls, and Bergmann's face looked grimly out from under it,
with the expression of an emperor taken captive
and guyed by the rebellious mob. Ashmeade,
of course, wore neither hat nor coat. He carried a slim umbrella, perfectly rolled. Outside,
Chatsworth's Rolls Royce, complete with chauf-
feur, was waiting—all light gray, to match his
own loose-fitting, well-cut clothes.

"Better get plenty of sleep tonight, Isherwood," he advised me graciously. "We're going
to work you hard."

Ashmeade said nothing. He smiled, and followed Chatsworth into the car.

Bergmann paused, took my hand. A smile of
extraordinary charm, of intimacy, came over
his face. He was standing very close to me.

"Good-bye, Mr. Isherwood," he said, in German. "I shall call you tomorrow morning." His
voice dropped; he looked deeply, affectionate-
ly, into my eyes. "I am sure we shall be very
happy together. You know, already, I feel absolutely no shame before you. We are like two
married men who meet in a whorehouse."

When I got home, my mother and Richard were in the drawing room waiting for me.

"Well!"

"Any success?"

"What was it like?"

"Did you meet him?"

I dropped into a chair. "Yes," I said, "I met him."

"And—is everything all right?"

"How do you mean, all right?"

"Are you going to take the job?"

"I don't know.... Well, yes ... Yes, I suppose I am."

One of Chatsworth's underlings had installed Bergmann in a service flat in Knightsbridge, not far from Hyde Park Corner. I found him there next morning, at the top of several steep flights of stairs. Even before we could see each other, he began to hail me from above. "Come up! Higher! Higher! Courage! Not yet! Where are you? Don't weaken! Aha! At last *Servus*, my friend!"

"Well?" I asked, as we shook hands. "How do you like it here?"

"Terrible!" Bergmann twinkled at me comically from under his black bush of eyebrow.

33

"It's an inferno! You have made the *as*-cent to hell."

This morning, he was no longer an emperor but an old clown, shock-headed, in his gaudy silk dressing gown. Tragi-comic, like all clowns, when you see them resting backstage after the show.

He laid his hand on my arm. "First, tell me one thing, please. Is your whole city as horrible as this?"

"Horrible? Why, this is the best part of it! Wait till you see our slums, and the suburbs."

Bergmann grinned. "You console me enormously."

He led the way into the flat. The small living room was tropically hot, under a heavy cloud of cigarette smoke. It reeked of fresh paint. The whole place was littered with clothes, papers and books, in explosive disorder, like the debris around a volcano.

Bergmann called, "Mademoiselle!" and a girl came out of the inner room. She had fair smooth hair, brushed plainly back from her temples, and a quiet oval face, which would have looked pretty, if her chin hadn't been too pointed. She wore rimless glasses and the wrong shade of lipstick. She was dressed in the neat jacket and skirt of a stenographer.

"Dorothy, I introduce you to Mr. Isherwood. Dorothy is my secretary, the most beautiful of all the gifts given me by the munificent Mr. Chatsworth. You see, Dorothy, Mr. Isherwood is the good Virgil who has come to guide me through this Anglo-Saxon comedy."

Dorothy smiled the smile of a new secretary—a bit bewildered still, but prepared for anything in the way of lunatic employers.

"And please suppress that fire," Bergmann added. "It definitely kills me."

Dorothy knelt down and turned off the gas fire, which had been roaring away in a corner. "Do you want me now," she asked, very businesslike, "or shall I be getting on with the letters?"

"We always want you, my darling. Without you, we could not exist for one moment. You are our Beatrice. But first, Mr. Virgil and I have to become acquainted. Or rather, he must become acquainted with me. For, you see," Bergmann continued, as Dorothy left the room, "I know everything about you already."

"You do?"

"Certainly. Everything that is important. Wait. I shall show you something."

Raising his forefinger, smilingly, to indicate that I must be patient, he began to rummage among the clothes and scattered papers. I watched with growing curiosity, as Bergmann's search became increasingly furious. Now and then, he would discover some object, evidently not the right one, hold it up before him for a moment, like a nasty-smelling dead rat, and toss it aside again with a snort of disgust or some exclamation such as "Abominable!" "*Scheusslich!*" "Too silly for words!" I watched him unearth, in this way, a fat black notebook, a shaving mirror, a bottle of hair tonic and an abdominal belt. Finally, under a pile of shirts, he found a copy of *Mein Kampf* which he kissed, before throwing it into the wastepaper basket. "I love him!" he told me, making a wry, comical face.

The search spread into the bedroom. I could hear him plunging about, snorting and breathing hard, as I stood by the mantelpiece, looking at the photographs of a large, blonde, humorous woman and a thin, dark, rather frightened girl. Next, the bathroom was explored. A couple of wet towels were flung out into the passage. Then Bergmann uttered a triumphant "Aha!" He strode back into the living room, waving a book above his head. It was my novel, *The Memorial*.

"So! Here we are! You see? I read it at

midnight. And again this morning, in my bath."

I was absurdly pleased and flattered. "Well," I tried to sound casual, "how did you like it?"

"I found it grandiose."

"It ought to have been much better. I'm afraid I ..."

"You are wrong," Bergmann told me, quite severely. He began to turn the pages. "This scene—he tries to make a suicide. It is genial." He frowned solemnly, as if daring me to contradict him. "This I find clearly genial."

I laughed and blushed. Bergmann watched me, smiling, like a proud parent who listens to his son being praised by the headmaster. Then he patted me on the shoulder.

"Look, if you do not believe me. I will show you. This I wrote this morning, after reading your book." He began to fumble in his pockets. As there were only seven of them, it didn't take him long. He pulled out a crumpled sheet of paper. "My first poem in English. To an English poet."

I took it and read:

When I am a boy, my mother tells to me
It is lucky to wake up when the morning is
    bright

And first of all hear a lark sing.

Now I am not longer a boy, and I wake.
The morning is dark.
I hear a bird singing with unknown name
In a strange country language, but it is luck, I
     think.

Who is he, this singer, who does not fear the
     gray city?
Will they drown him soon, the poor Shelley?
Will Byron's hangmen teach him how one
     limps?
I hope they will not, because he makes me
     happy.

"Why," I said, "it's beautiful!"

"You like it?" Bergmann was so delighted
that he began rubbing his hands. "But you
must correct the English, please."

"Certainly not. I like it the way it is."

"Already I think I have a feeling for the
language," said Bergmann, with modest satisfaction. "I shall write many English poems."

"May I keep this one?"

"Really? You want it?" he beamed. "Then I
shall inscribe it for you."

He took out his fountain pen and wrote: "For

Christopher, from Friedrich, his fellow prisoner."

I laid the poem carefully on the mantelpiece. It seemed to be the only safe place in the room. "Is this your wife?" I asked, looking at the photographs.

"Yes. And that is Inge, my daughter. You like her?"

"She has beautiful eyes."

"She is a pianist. Very talented."

"Are they in Vienna?"

"Unfortunately. Yes. I am most anxious for them. Austria is no longer safe. The plague is spreading. I wished them to come with me, but my wife has to look after her mother. It's not so easy." Bergmann sighed deeply. Then, with a sharp glance at me, "You are not married." It sounded like an accusation.

"How did you know?"

"I know these things. . . . You live with your parents?"

"With my mother and brother. My father's dead."

Bergmann grunted and nodded. He was like a doctor who finds his most pessimistic diagnosis is confirmed. "You are a typical mother's son. It is the English tragedy."

I laughed. "Quite a lot of Englishmen do get married, you know."

"They marry their mothers. It is a disaster. It will lead to the destruction of Europe."

"I must say, I don't quite see . . ."

"It will lead definitely to the destruction of Europe. I have written the first chapters of a novel about this. It is called *The Diary of an Etonian Oedipus.*" Bergmann suddenly gave me a charming smile. "But do not worry. We shall change all that."

"All right," I grinned. "I won't worry."

Bergmann lit a cigarette, and blew a cloud of smoke into which he almost disappeared.

"And now," he announced, "the horrible but unavoidable moment has come when we have to talk about this crime we are about to commit: this public outrage, this enormous nuisance, this scandal, this blasphemy. . . . You have read the original script?"

"They sent a messenger round with it, last night."

"And . . . ?" Bergmann watched me keenly, waiting for my answer.

"It's even worse than I expected."

"Marvelous! Excellent! You see, I am such a horrible old sinner that nothing is ever as *bad* as I expect. But you are surprised. You are shocked. That is because you are innocent. It is this innocence which I need absolutely to help me, the innocence of Alyosha Karamazov. I shall proceed to corrupt you. I shall teach you everything from the very beginning. . . . Do you know what the film is?" Bergmann cupped his hands, lovingly, as if around an exquisite flower. "The film is an infernal machine. Once it is ignited and set in motion, it revolves with an enormous dynamism. It cannot pause. It cannot apologize. It cannot retract anything. It cannot wait for you to understand it. It cannot explain itself. It simply ripens to its inevitable explosion. This explosion we have to prepare, like anarchists, with the utmost ingenuity and malice. . . . While you were in Germany did you ever see *Frau Nussbaum's letzter Tag?*"

"Indeed I did. Three or four times."

Bergmann beamed. "I directed it."

"No? Really?"

"You didn't know?"

"I'm afraid I never read the credits. . . . Why, that was one of the best German pictures!"

Bergmann nodded, delighted, accepting this as a matter of course. "You must tell that to Umbrella."

"Umbrella?"

"The Beau Brummel who appeared to us yesterday at lunch."

"Oh, Ashmeade . . ."

Bergmann looked concerned. "He is a great friend of yours?"

"No," I grinned. "Not exactly."

"You see, this umbrella of his I find extremely symbolic. It is the British respectability which thinks: 'I have my traditions, and they will protect me. Nothing unpleasant, nothing ungentlemanly can possibly happen within my private park.' This respectable umbrella is the Englishman's magic wand, with which he will try to wave Hitler out of existence. When Hitler declines rudely to disappear, the Englishman will open his umbrella and say, 'After all, what do I care for a little rain?' But the rain will be a rain of bombs and blood. The umbrella is not bomb-proof."

"Don't underrate the umbrella," I said. "It has often been used successfully, by governesses against bulls. It has a very sharp point."

"You are wrong. The umbrella is useless. . . . Do you know Goethe?"

"Only a little."

"Wait. I shall read you something. Wait. Wait."

"The whole *beauty* of the film," I announced to my mother and Richard next morning at breakfast, "is that it has a certain fixed *speed*. The way you see it is mechanically conditioned. I mean, take a painting—you can just glance at it, or you can stare at the left-hand top corner for half an hour. Same thing with a book. The author can't stop you from skimming it, or starting at the last chapter and reading backwards. The point is, you choose your approach. When you go into a cinema, it's different. There's the film, and you have to look at it as the director wants you to look at it. He makes his points, one after another, and he allows you a certain number of seconds or minutes to grasp each one. If you miss anything, he won't repeat himself, and he won't stop to explain. He can't. He's started something, and he has to go through with it. . . . You see, the film is really like a sort of infernal machine . . ."

I stopped abruptly, with my hands in the air. I had caught myself in the middle of one of Bergmann's most characteristic gestures.

I had always had a pretty good opinion of myself as a writer. But, during those first days with Bergmann, it was lowered considerably. I had flattered myself that I had imagination, that I could invent dialogue, that I could develop a character. I had believed that I could describe almost anything, just as a competent artist can draw you an old man's face, or a table, or a tree.

Well, it seemed that I was wrong.

The period is early twentieth century, some time before the 1914 war. It is a warm spring evening in the Vienna Prater. The dancehalls are lighted up. The coffee houses are full. The bands blare. Fireworks are bursting above the trees. The swings are swinging. The roundabouts are revolving. There are freak shows, gypsies telling fortunes, boys playing the concertina. Crowds of people are eating, drinking beer, wandering along the paths beside the river. The drunks sing noisily. The lovers, arm in arm, stroll whispering in the shadow of the elms and the silver poplars.

There is a girl named Toni, who sells violets. Everybody knows her, and she has a word for everybody. She laughs and jokes as she offers the flowers. An officer tries to kiss her; she slips away from him good-humoredly. An old lady has lost her dog; she is sympathetic. An indignant, tyrannical gentleman is looking for his daughter; Toni knows where she is, and with whom, but she won't tell.

Then, as she wanders down the alleys carrying her basket, light-hearted and fancy-free, she comes face to face with a handsome boy in the dress of a student. He tells her, truthfully, that his name is Rudolf. But he is not what he seems. He is really the Crown Prince of Borodania.

All this I was to describe. "Do not concern yourself with the shots," Bergmann had told me. "Just write dialogue. Create atmosphere. Give the camera something to listen to and look at."

I couldn't. I couldn't. My impotence nearly reduced me to tears. It was all so simple, surely? There is Toni's father, for instance. He is fat and jolly, and he has a stall where he sells *Wiener Wuerstchen*. He talks to his customers. He talks to Toni. Toni talks to the customers. They reply. It is all very gay, amusing, delightful. But what the hell do they actually say?

I didn't know. I couldn't write it. That was the brutal truth—I couldn't draw a table. I tried to take refuge in my pride. After all, this was movie work, hack work. It was something essentially false, cheap, vulgar. It was beneath me. I ought never to have become involved in it, under the influence of Bergmann's dangerous charm, and for the sake of the almost incredible twenty pounds a week which Imperial Bulldog was prepared, quite as a matter of course, to pay me. I was betraying my art. No wonder it was so difficult.

Nonsense. I didn't really believe that, either, It isn't vulgar to be able to make people talk. An old man selling sausages isn't vulgar, except in the original meaning of the word, "belonging to the common people." Shakespeare would have known how he spoke. Tolstoy would have known. I didn't know because, for all my parlor socialism, I was a snob. I didn't know how anybody spoke, except public-school boys and neurotic bohemians.

I fell back, in my despair, upon memories of other movies. I tried to be smart, facetious. I made involved, wordy jokes. I wrote a page of dialogue which led nowhere and only succeeded in establishing the fact that an anonymous minor character was having an affair with somebody else's wife. As for Rudolf, the incognito Prince, he talked like the lowest common demoninator of all the worst musical comedies I had ever seen. I hardly dared to show my wretched attempts to Bergmann at all.

He read them through with furrowed brows and a short profound grunt; but he didn't seem either dismayed or surprised. "Let me tell you something, Master," he began, as he dropped my manuscript casually into the wastepaper basket, "the film is a symphony. Each movement is written in a certain key. There is a note which has to be chosen and struck immediately. It is characteristic of the whole. It commands the attention."

Sitting very close to me, and pausing only to draw long breaths from his cigarette, he started to describe the opening sequence. It was astounding. Everything came to life. The trees began to tremble in the evening breeze, the music was heard, the roundabouts were set in motion. And the people talked. Bergmann improvised their conversation, partly in German, partly in ridiculous English; and it was vivid and real. His eyes sparkled, his gestures grew more exaggerated, he mimicked, he clowned. I began to laugh. Bergmann smiled delightedly at his own invention. It was all so simple, so effective, so obvious. Why hadn't I thought of it myself?

Bergmann gave me a little pat on the shoulder. "It's nice, isn't it?"

"It's wonderful! I'll note that down before I forget."

Immediately, he was very serious. "No, no. It is wrong. All wrong, I only wanted to give you some idea ... No, that won't do. Wait. We must consider ..."

Clouds followed the sunshine. Bergmann scowled grimly as he passed into philosophical analysis. He gave me ten excellent reasons why the whole thing was impossible. They, too, were obvious. Why hadn't I thought of them? Bergmann sighed. "It's not so easy ..." He lit another cigarette. "Not so easy," he muttered. "Wait. Wait. Let us see ..."

He rose and paced the carpet, breathing hard, his hands folded severely behind his back, his face shut against the outside world, implacably, like a prison door. Then a thought struck him. He stopped, amused by it. He smiled.

"You know what my wife tells me when I have these difficulties? 'Friedrich,' she says, 'Go and write your poems. When I have cooked the dinner, I will invent this idiotic story for you. After all, prostitution is a woman's business.'"

That was what Bergmann was like on his good days; the days when I was Alyosha Karamazov, or, as he told Dorothy, like Balaam's ass, "who *once* said a marvelous line." My incompetence merely stimulated him to more brilliant flights of imagination. He sparkled with epigrams, he beamed, he really amazed himself. On such days, we suited each other perfectly. Bergmann didn't really need a collaborator at all. But he needed stimulation and sympathy; he needed someone he could talk German to. He needed an audience.

His wife wrote to him every day, Inge two or three times a week. He read me extracts from their letters, full of household, theatrical and political gossip; and these led to anecdotes, about Inge's first concert, about his mother-in-law, about German and Austrian actors, and the plays and films he had directed. He would spend a whole hour describing how he had produced *Macbeth* in Dresden, with masks, in the style of a Greek tragedy. A morning would go by while he recited his poems, or told me of his last days in Berlin, in the spring of that year, when the Storm Troopers were roving the streets like bandits, and his wife had saved him from several dangerous situations by a quick answer or a joke. Although Bergmann was an Austrian, he had been advised to give up his job and leave Germany in a hurry. They had lost most of their money in consequence. "And so, when Chatsworth's offer came, you see, I could not afford to refuse. There was no alternative. I had my doubts about this artificial

Violet, from the very first. Even across half of Europe, it didn't smell so good. . . . Never mind, I said to myself. Here is a problem. Every problem has its solution. We will do what we can. We will not despair. Who knows? Perhaps, after all, we shall present Mr. Chatsworth with a charming nosegay, a nice little surprise."

Bergmann wanted all my time, all my company, all my attention. During those first weeks, our working day steadily increased in length, until I had to make a stand and insist on going home to supper. He seemed determined to possess me utterly. He pursued me with questions, about my friends, my interests, my habits, my love life. The weekends, especially, were the object of his endless, jealous curiosity. What did I do? Whom did I see? Did I live like a monk? "Is it Mr. W. H. you seek, or the Dark Lady of the Sonnets?" But I was equally obstinate. I wouldn't tell him. I teased him with smiles and hints.

Foiled, he turned his attention to Dorothy. Younger and less experienced, she was no match for his inquisitiveness. One morning, I arrived to find her in tears. She rose abruptly and hurried into the next room. "She has her struggle," Bergmann told me, with a certain grim satisfaction. "It's not so easy." Dorothy, it appeared, had a boy friend, an older man, who was married. He didn't seem able to make up his mind which of the two women he liked better; just now, he had gone back to his wife. His name was Clem. He was a car salesman. He had taken Dorothy to Brighton for weekends. Dorothy also had a lover of her own age, a radio engineer, nice and steady, who wanted to marry her. But the radio engineer lacked glamour; he couldn't compete with the fatal appeal of Clem, who wore a little black mustache.

Bergmann's interest in all this was positively ghoulish. In addition, he knew everything about Dorothy's father, another sinister influence, and about her aunt, who worked at an undertaker's, and was having an affair with her brother-in-law. At first, I could hardly believe that Dorothy had really brought herself to reveal such intimate details, and suspected Bergmann of having invented the whole story. She seemed such a shy, reserved girl. But soon they were actually speaking of Clem in my presence. When Dorothy cried, Bergmann would pat her on the shoulder, like God Himself, and murmur, "That's all right, my child. Nothing to do. It will pass."

He was fond of lecturing me on Love. "When

a woman is awakened, when she gets the man she wants, she is amazing, amazing. You have no idea ... Sensuality is a whole separate world. What we see on the outside, what comes up to the surface—it's nothing. Love is like a mine. You go deeper and deeper. There are passages, caves, whole strata. You discover entire geological eras. You find things, little objects, which enable you to reconstruct her life, her other lovers, things she does not even know about herself, things you must never tell her that you know ...

"You see," Bergmann continued, "women are absolutely necessary to a man; especially to a man who lives in ideas, in the creation of moods and thoughts. He needs them, like bread. I do not mean for the coitus; that is not so important, at my age. One lives more in the fantasy. But one needs their aura, their ambience, their perfume. Women always recognize a man who wants this thing from them. They feel it at once, and they come to him, like horses." Bergmann paused, grinning. "You see, I am an old Jewish Socrates who preaches to the Youth. One day, they will give me the hemlock."

In the hot little room, our life together seemed

curiously isolated. The three of us formed a self-contained world, independent of London, of Europe, of 1933. Dorothy, the representative of Woman, did her best to keep the home in some kind of order, but her efforts were not very successful. Her schemes for arranging Bergmann's huge litter of papers only caused worse confusion. As he could never describe exactly what it was that he was looking for, she could never tell him where she had put it. This sent him into frenzies of frustration. "Terrible, terrible. This definitely kills me. Too idiotic for words." And he would relapse into grumpy silence.

Then there was the problem of meals. The house had a restaurant service, theoretically. It could produce bitter coffee, very strong black tea, congealed eggs, sodden toast and a gluey chop, followed by some nameless kind of yellow pudding. The food took an almost incredible time to arrive. As Bergmann said, when you ordered breakfast, it was best to ask for what you wanted at lunch, because it would be four hours before you got it. So we lived chiefly on cigarettes.

At least twice a week, there was a Black Day. I would enter the flat to find Bergmann in complete despair. He hadn't slept all night, the

53

story was hopeless, Dorothy was crying. The best way of dealing with this situation was to make Bergmann come out with me to lunch. Our nearest restaurant was a big gloomy place on the top floor of a department store. We ate early, when there were very few other customers, sitting together at a table in the darkest corner, next to a rather sinister grandfather clock, which reminded Bergmann of the story by Edgar Allan Poe.

"It ticks every moment," he told me. "Death comes nearer. Syphilis. Poverty. Consumption. Cancer discovered too late. My art no good, a failure, a damn flop. War. Poison gas. We are dying with our heads together in the oven."

And then he would begin to describe the coming war. The attack on Vienna, Prague, London and Paris, without warning, by thousands of planes, dropping bombs filled with deadly bacilli; the conquest of Europe in a week; the subjugation of Asia, Africa, the Americas; the massacre of the Jews, the execution of intellectuals, the herding of non-Nordic women into enormous state brothels; the burning of paintings and books, the grinding of statues into powder; the mass sterilization of the unfit, mass murder of the elderly, mass conditioning of the young; the reduction of

France and the Balkan countries to wilderness, in order to make national parks for the Hitler Jugend; the establishment of Brown Art, Brown Literature, Brown Music, Brown Philosophy, Brown Science and the Hitler Religion, with its Vatican at Munich and its Lourdes at Berchtesgaden: a cult based upon the most complex system of dogmas concerning the real nature of the Fuehrer, the utterances of *Mein Kampf*, the ten thousand Bolshevist heresies, the sacrament of Blood and Soil, and upon elaborate rituals of mystic union with the Homeland, involving human sacrifice and the baptism of steel.

"All these people," Bergmann continued, "will be dead. All of them . . . No, there is one . . ." He pointed to a fat, inoffensive man sitting alone in a distant corner. "He will survive. He is the kind that will do anything, anything to be allowed to live. He will invite the conquerors to his home, force his wife to cook for them and serve the dinner on his bended knees. He will denounce his mother. He will offer his sister to a common soldier. He will act as a spy in prisons. He will spit on the Sacrament. He will hold down his daughter while they rape her. And, as a reward for this, he will be given a job as bootblack in a public lavatory, and he will lick the dirt from people's shoes with his tongue..." Bergmann shook his head sadly. "Too bad. I do not envy him."

This kind of talk had a strange effect on me. Like all my friends, I said I believed that a European war was coming soon. I believed it as one believes that one will die, and yet I didn't believe. For the coming war was as unreal to me as death itself. It was unreal because I couldn't imagine anything beyond it; I refused to imagine anything; just as a spectator refuses to imagine what is behind the scenery in a theatre. The outbreak of war, like the moment of death, crossed my perspective of the future like a wall; it marked the instant, total end of my imagined world. I thought about this wall from time to time, with acute depression and a flutter of fear at the solar plexus. Then, again, I forgot or ignored it. Also, just as when one thinks of one's own death, I secretly whispered to myself, "Who knows? Maybe we shall get around it somehow. Maybe it will never happen."

Bergmann's apocalyptic pictures of universal doom made the prospect of war more unreal than ever, and so they never failed to cheer me up. I suppose they worked like that for him, too, probably that was why he dwelt upon them so gleefully. And, while he was in the midst of the horrors, his glance around the room generally discovered a girl or woman who interested him, and diverted the stream of his imagination toward more agreeable subjects.

His favorite was the manageress of the restaurant, a handsome blonde with a very sweet motherly smile, about thirty years old. Bergmann approved of her highly. "I have only to look at her," he told me, "to know that she is satisfied. Deeply satisfied. Some man has made her happy. For her, there is no longer any search. She has found what we are all looking for. She understands all of us. She does not need books, or theories, or philosophy, or priests. She understands Michelangelo, Beethoven, Christ, Lenin—even Hitler. And she is afraid of nothing, nothing. . . . Such a woman is my religion."

The manageress would always have a special smile for Bergmann when we came in; and, during the meal, she would walk over to our table and ask if everything was all right. "Everything is all right, my darling," Bergmann would reply, "thanks to God, but chiefly to you. You restore our confidence in ourselves."

I don't know exactly what the manageress made of this, but she smiled, in an amused, kindly way. She really was very nice. "You see?" Bergmann would turn to me, after she had gone. "We understand each other perfectly."

And so, our confidence restored by *das ewige Weibliche,* we went back refreshed to tend the poor little *Prater Violet,* wilting in the suffocating atmosphere of our flat.

Meanwhile, in Berlin, the proceedings of the Reichstag Fire Trial continued through October, November and into the first two weeks of December. Bergmann followed them passionately. "Do you know what he said yesterday?" he would frequently ask me, when I arrived in the morning for work. "He," of course, was Dimitrov. I did know, having read the newspaper as eagerly as Bergmann himself, but I wouldn't, for the world, have spoiled the performance which followed.

Bergmann enacted the entire drama and represented all the characters. He was Dr. Buenger, the testy, embarrassed President of the Court. He was van der Lubbe, doped and apathetic, with sunken head. He was earnest, harassed Torgler. He was Goering, the straddling military bully, and Goebbels, lizardlike, crooked and adroit. He was fiery Popov and stolid Tanev. And, in the biggest way, he was Dimitrov himself.

Bergmann actually became Dimitrov, with his furiously untidy hair, his grim ironic slit of a mouth, his large gestures, his flashing eyes.

"Is the Herr Reichsminister aware," he thundered, "that those who possess this alleged criminal mentality are today controlling the destinies of a sixth part of the world, namely the Soviet Union—the greatest and best land on earth?"

Then, as Goering, bull-necked, infuriated, he bellowed, "I'll tell you what I'm aware of! I'm aware that you're a communist spy who came to Germany to set the Reichstag on fire. In my eyes, you're nothing but a dirty crook, who ought to be hanging on the gallows!"

Bergmann smiled, a faint, terrible smile. Like a toreador, who never takes his eyes from the enraged and wounded bull, he asked softly, "You are very afraid of my questions, aren't you, Herr Minister?"

Bergmann's face contorted, bulged, seemed to swell into an apoplectic clot of blood. His hand shot out. He yelled like a lunatic, "Get out of here, you crook!"

Bergmann bowed slightly, with ironic dignity. He half turned, as if to withdraw. Then he

paused. His eye fell upon the imagined figure
of van der Lubbe. His hand was raised, slowly,
in a great, historic gesture. He addressed all
Europe:

"There stands the miserable Faust. . . . But
where is Mephistopheles?"

Then he made his exit.

"You wait!" Bergmann-Goering roared after
the retreating figure. "You wait till I get you
out of the power of this Court!"

Another scene, which Dorothy and I would
often persuade Bergmann to repeat, was the
moment when van der Lubbe is cross-
examined. He stands before his accusers, with
his huge stooped shoulders and hanging hands,
the chin sunken on the chest. He is scarcely
human—a wretched, clumsy, tormented animal. The President tries to make him look up.
He does not move. The Interpreter tries. Dr.
Seuffert tries. There is no response. Then, suddenly, with the harsh authority of an animal
trainer, Helldorf barks out, "Head up, man!
Quick!"

The head jerks up at once, automatically, as
if in obedience to some deeply hidden memory.
The clouded eyes wander around the courtroom. Are they searching for somebody? A
faint gleam of recognition seems to flicker in

them for a moment. And then van der Lubbe begins to laugh. This is really horrible, indecent, terrifying. The heavy body quivers and heaves with noiseless laughter, as if shaken by its death agony. Van der Lubbe laughs and laughs, silently, blindly, his mouth open and dribbling, like an idiot's. Then, with equal suddenness, the paroxysm ceases. Again, the head falls forward. The grotesque figure stands motionless, guarding its secret, unapproachable as the dead.

"Goodness!" Dorothy would exclaim, with a shiver. "I'm glad I'm not over there! It gives you the creeps, just to think about it. Those Nazis aren't human."

"You are wrong, darling," Bergmann told her, seriously. "That is how they wish you to imagine them, as unconquerable monsters. But they are human, very human, in their weakness. We must not fear them. We must understand them. It is absolutely necessary to understand them, or we are all lost."

Now that Bergmann had become Dimitrov, he was obliged to abandon a great deal of his cynicism. It was no longer in character. Dimitrov had to have a cause to fight for, to make speeches about. And the cause turned out to be *Prater Violet.*

We were at work on the sequence in which Rudolf loses his future kingdom of Borodania through a palace revolution. A wicked uncle deposes his father and seizes the throne. Rudolf returns to Vienna, a penniless exile. He is now, in reality, the poor student he pretended to be at the beginning of the story. But Toni, naturally, refuses to believe this. She has been deceived once already. She has trusted him, she has loved him, and he has left her. (Unwillingly, of course; and only because his faithful chamberlain, Count Rosanoff, reminds him with tears of his duty to the Borodanians.) So Rudolf pleads in vain; and Toni angrily dismisses him as an impostor.

We had been through the usual procedure. I had made my lazy, half-hearted attempt at a first draft. Bergmann had put it aside with his brief grunt. And now, with his usual brilliance and wealth of gesture, he had gone over the story for the second time.

But it didn't work. I was feeling temperamental and sulky that day, chiefly because I had a bad cold. My conscience had driven me to Bergmann's flat, and I felt that my sacrifice wasn't being properly appreciated. I had expected to be fussed over and sent home again.

"It's no good," I told him.

Bergmann was belligerent at once. "Why is it no good?"

"I'm afraid it just doesn't interest me."

Bergmann gave a terrible snort. I seldom defied him like this. But I was in a thoroughly obstructive mood. I didn't care if I got fired. I didn't care what happened.

"It's such a bore," I said brutally. "It's so completely unreal. It has no relation to anything that ever happened anywhere. I can't believe a word of it."

For a whole minute, he didn't answer. He paced the carpet, grunting. Dorothy, from her seat at the typewriter, watched him nervously. I expected a major volcanic eruption.

Then Bergmann came right up to me.

"You are wrong," he said.

I looked him in the eye, and forced a smile. But I didn't say anything. I wouldn't give him an opening.

"Totally and principally wrong. It is not uninteresting. It is not unreal. It is of the very greatest interest. It is highly contemporary. And it is of enormous psychological and political significance."

I was startled right out of my sulks.

"Political?" I laughed. "Why, really, Friedrich! How on earth do you make that out?"

"It is political." Bergmann swept into the attack. "And the reason you refuse to see this, the reason you pretend it is uninteresting, is that it directly concerns yourself."

"I must say, I . . ."

"Listen!" Bergmann interrupted imperiously. "The dilemma of Rudolf is the dilemma of the would-be revolutionary writer or artist, all over Europe. This writer is not to be confused with the true proletarian writer, such as we find in Russia. His economic background is bourgeois. He is accustomed to comfort, a nice home, the care of a devoted slave who is his mother and also his jailer. From the safety and comfort of his home, he permits himself the luxury of a romantic interest in the proletariat. He comes among the workers under false pretenses, and in disguise. He flirts with Toni, the girl of the working class. But it is only a damn lousy act, a heartless masquerade . . ."

"Well, if you like to put it in that way. . . . But what about . . . ?"

"Listen! Suddenly Rudolf's home collapses, security collapses. The investments which built his comfortable life are made worthless by inflation. His mother has to scrub doorsteps. The young artist-prince, with all his fine ideas, has to face grim reality. The play becomes bitter earnest. His relation to the proletariat is romantic no longer. He now has to make a choice. He is declassed, and he must find a new class. Does he really love Toni? Did his beautiful words mean anything? If so, he must prove that they did. Otherwise..."

"Yes, that's all very well, but..."

"This symbolic fable," Bergmann continued, with sadistic relish, "is particularly disagreeable to you, because it represents your deepest fear, the nightmare of your own class. In England, the economic catastrophe has not yet occurred. The pound wavered, but it did not utterly fall. Inflation still lies ahead of the English bourgeoisie, but you know in your heart that it is coming, as it came to Germany. And, when it comes, you will have to choose...."

"How do you mean, choose?"

"The declassed intellectual has two choices. If his love for Toni is sincere, if he is loyal to his artistic traditions, the great liberal-revolutionary traditions of the nineteenth century, then he will know where he belongs. He will know how to align himself. He will know who are his real friends and his real enemies." (My eye caught Dorothy's. She was watching us blankly, for Bergmann, as he usually did when excited, had started to talk in German.)

"Unfortunately, however, he does not always make this choice. Indeed, he seldom makes it. He is unable to cut himself free, sternly, from the bourgeois dream of the Mother, that fatal and comforting dream. He wants to crawl back into the economic safety of the womb. He hates the paternal, revolutionary tradition, which reminds him of his duty as its son. His pretended love for the masses was only a flirtation, after all. He now prefers to join the ranks of the dilettante nihilists, the bohemian outlaws, who believe in nothing, except their own ego, who exist only to kill, to torture, to destroy, to make everyone as miserable as themselves . . ."

"In other words, I'm a Nazi and you're my father?"

We both laughed.

"I only try to analyze certain tendencies," said Bergmann.

"Nevertheless," he added, "there are times when I feel gravely worried about you."

Bergmann worried not only about me, but about the whole of England. Wherever he went, he kept a sharp lookout for what he called "significant phenomena." A phenomenon, I soon discovered, could be practically anything. The fog, for instance. Like nearly all Middle-Europeans, he was convinced that fog was our normal weather throughout the year. I would have been sorry to disappoint him; and, as luck would have it, there were several quite thick fogs that winter. Bergmann seemed to imagine that they covered not only London but the entire island; thereby accounting for all our less agreeable racial characteristics, our insularity, our hypocrisy, our political muddling, our prudery and our refusal to face facts. "It is the English themselves who have created this fog. They feed upon it, like a kind of bitter soup which fills them with illusions. It is their national costume, clothing the enormous nakedness of the slums and the scandal of unjust ownership. It is also the jungle within which Jack the Ripper goes about his business of murder in the elegant overcoat of a member of the Stock Exchange."

We started making sightseeing excursions together. Bergmann showed me London: the London he had already created for himself in his own imagination, the dark, intricate, sinister town of Dickens, the old German silent movies, Wedekind and Brecht. He was always the guide, and I the tourist. Whenever I asked where we were going, he would say, "Wait," or "You will see." Often, I think he hadn't the least idea, until we actually arrived.

We visited the Tower, where Bergmann lectured me on English history, comparing the reign of the Tudors to the Hitler regime. He took it for granted that Bacon wrote the Shakespearean plays, in order to make political propaganda, and that Queen Elizabeth was a man. He even had a further theory that Essex was beheaded because he threatened the Monarch with revelations of their homosexual intrigue. I had some difficulty in getting him out of the Bloody Tower, where he was inspired to a lurid reconstruction of the murder of the Little Princes, amazing the other visitors, who merely saw a stocky, shock-headed, middle-aged man pleading for his life to an invisible assassin, in German, with theatrical falsetto accents.

At the Zoo, he identified a baboon, a giraffe and a dromedary with three of our leading politicians, and reproached them publicly for their crimes. In the National Gallery, he explained, with reference to the Rembrandt portraits, his theory of camera angles and the lighting of close-ups, so loudly and convincingly that he drew a crowd away from one of the official lecturers, who was naturally rather annoyed.

Sometimes he persuaded me to go out with him at night. This, at the end of a long day, was very exhausting. But the streets fascinated him, and he never seemed tired or wished to return home. It was embarrassing, too. Bergmann spoke to anybody whose face happened to interest him, with the directness of a child; or he talked about them to me, like a lecturer, so that they were sure to overhear him. One evening, in the bus, there were two lovers. The girl was sitting just in front of us; the young man stood beside her, holding the strap. Bergmann was delighted with them. "See how he stands? They do not even look at each other. They might be strangers. Yet they keep touching, as if by accident. Now watch: their lips are moving. That is how two people talk when they are very happy and alone, in the darkness. Already they are lying in each other's arms in bed. Good night, my dears. We shall not intrude upon your secrets."

Bergmann talked to taxi-drivers, to medical students in bars, to elderly colonels returning from their clubs, to clergymen, to Piccadilly tarts, to the boys who hung around the medallion of W. S. Gilbert on the Embankment. Nobody seemed to mind, or even to misunderstand his intentions. I envied him his freedom—the freedom of a foreigner. I could have done the same thing, myself, in Vienna or

Berlin. With a foreigner's luck, or intuition, he nearly always succeeded in picking out the unusual individual from the average type: a constable who did water colors, a beggar who knew classical Greek. And this betrayed him into a foreigner's generalizations. In London, all policemen paint, all the scholars are starving.

The year was drawing to an end. The newspapers were full of optimism. Things were looking up; this Christmas was to be the greatest ever. Hitler talked only of peace. The Disarmament Conference had broken down. The British Government didn't want isolation; equally, it didn't want to promise military aid to France. When people planned their next summer's holiday in Europe, they remembered to add, "If Europe's still there." It was like the superstition of touching wood.

Just before Christmas, Bergmann and I went down to Brighton for the day. It was the only time we ever left London together. I remember this as one of the most depressing experiences of my life. Behind high clouds of white fog, the wintry sun made a pale splash of gold, far out on the oyster-gray surface of the Channel. We walked along the pier and stopped to watch a

young man in plus-fours with a fair mangy
mustache, who was hitting a punch-ball. "He
can't ring the bell," I said. "None of them can
ring it," Bergmann answered somberly. "That
bell will never ring again. They're all done for.
Finished." Coming back in the Pullman car, the
sea air made us both doze. I had a peculiarly
vivid nightmare about Hitler Germany.

First of all, I dreamed that I was in a courtroom. This, I knew, was a political trial. Some
communists were being sentenced to death.
The State Prosecutor was a hard-faced, middle-
aged, blonde woman, with her hair twisted into
a knot on the back of her head. She stood up,
gripping one of the accused men by his coat
collar, and marched him down the room
toward the judge's desk. As they advanced, she
drew a revolver and shot the communist in the
back. His knees sagged and his chin fell forward; but she dragged him on, until they faced
the judge, and she cried, in a loud voice,
"Look! Here is the traitor!"

A girl was sitting beside me, among the
spectators. In some way, I was aware that she
was a hospital nurse by profession. As the
prosecutor held up the dying man, she rose and
ran out of the courtroom in tears. I followed
her, down passages and flights of steps, into a

cellar, where there were central-heating pipes. The cellar was fitted with bunks, like a barracks. The girl lay down on one of them, sobbing. And then several youths came in. I knew that they belonged to the Hitler Jugend; but, instead of uniforms, they wore bits of bearskin, with belts, helmets and swords, shoddy and theatrical-looking, such as supers might wear in a performance of "The Ring." Their partly naked bodies were covered with acne and skin rash, and they seemed tired and dispirited. They climbed into their bunks, without taking the least notice of the girl or of me.

Then I was walking up a steep, very narrow street. A Jew came running down toward me, with his wrists thrust into his overcoat pockets. I knew that this was because his hands had been shot off. He had to hide his injuries. If anybody saw them, he would be recognized and lynched.

At the top of the street, I found an old lady, dressed in a kind of uniform, French "horizon blue." She was sniveling and cursing to herself. It was she who had shot off the Jew's hands. She wanted to shoot him again; but her ammunition (which was, I noticed with surprise, only for a .22 rifle) lay scattered on the ground. She couldn't collect it, because she was blind.

Then I went into the British Embassy, where I was welcomed by a cheerful, fatuous, drawling young man, like Wodehouse's Bertie Wooster. He pointed out to me that the walls of the entrance hall were covered with post-impressionist and cubist paintings. "The Ambassador likes them," he explained. "I mean to say, a bit of contrast, what?"

Somehow, I couldn't bring myself to tell this dream to Bergmann. I wasn't in the mood for one of his elaborate and perhaps disagreeably personal interpretations. Also, I had a curious suspicion that he had put the whole thing, tele-pathically, into my head.

All these months, there hadn't been a single word from Chatsworth.

His silence was magnificent. It seemed to express the most generous kind of confidence. He was giving us an absolutely free hand. Or perhaps he was so busy that he had forgotten about us altogether.

I think he must have written *Prater Violet* on the first leaf of his 1934 calendar. For January had barely begun before we started to get telephone calls from the studio. How was the script coming along?

Bergmann went down to Imperial Bulldog to

see him, and came back in a state of considerable self-satisfaction. He gave me to understand that he had been exceedingly diplomatic. Chatsworth's stock rose. He was no longer a vulgarian, but a man of culture and insight. "He appreciates," said Bergmann, "how a director needs time to follow his ideas quietly and lovingly." Bergmann had told the story, no doubt with a most lavish display of gesture and intonation, and Chatsworth had seemed very pleased.

However, this didn't alter the fact that our script was still a torso, or at best, a living body with mechanical limbs. The final sequence, the whole episode of Toni's revenge on Rudolf with its happy ending, was still wishfully vague. Neither of us really liked the idea of her masquerade, in a blonde wig, as the famous opera singer. Not all Bergmann's histrionics, no amount of Freudian analysis or Marxian dialectic could make it anything but very silly.

And perhaps Chatsworth hadn't been so impressed, after all. Because now we started to have visits from Ashmeade. His approach was extremely tactful. It opened with what appeared to be a purely social call. "I happened to be passing," he told us, "so I thought I'd look in. Are you and Isherwood still on speaking terms?"

But Bergmann wasn't deceived. "The Secret Police are on our footprints," he said gloomily. "So . . . Now it begins."

Two days later, Ashmeade returned. This time, he was more frankly inquisitive. He wanted to know all about the last sequence. Bergmann went into his act; he had never been better. Ashmeade looked politely dubious.

Next morning, early, he was on the phone. "I've been thinking it over. I've just had an idea. Suppose Toni knew all the time that Rudolf was the Prince? I mean, right from the beginning."

"No, no, no!" cried Bergmann in despair. "Definitely not!"

When their conversation was over, he was furious. "They have given me this fashionable cretin, this elegant dwarf to sit on my back! Have we not enough burdens already? Here we are, breaking our heads off fighting for Truth!"

His anger, as always, subsided into philosophic doubt. He could never dismiss any suggestion, however fantastic, without hours of soul-searching. He groaned painfully. "Very well, let us see where this leads us. Wait. Wait. Let us see . . . How would it be if Toni . . . ?"

Another day was lost in speculation.

Ashmeade was indefatigable. Either he telephoned, or he came to visit us, every day. He never minded being snubbed, and his ideas abounded. Bergmann began to entertain the blackest suspicions.

"I see it all. This is a plot. It is a clear sabotage. This diplomatic Umbrella has his instructions. Chatsworth is playing with us. He has decided not to make the picture."

I was inclined to agree with him; and I couldn't altogether blame Chatsworth, either. No doubt, Bergmann's methods were leisurely. Perhaps they were conditioned by habits formed in the old silent days, when the director went into the studio and photographed everything within sight, finally revising his story in the cutting room by a process of selection and elimination. I was seriously afraid that Bergmann would soon reach a state of philosophic equilibrium, in which all possible solutions would seem equally attractive or unattractive, and that we should hang poised in potentiality, until the studio stopped sending us our checks.

Then, one morning, the telephone rang. It was Chatsworth's private secretary. (I recognized the voice which had introduced me to *Prater Violet,* on that last day of what I now looked back to as the pre-Bergmann period of my life.) Would we please both come to the studio as soon as possible, for a script conference?

Bergmann was very grim as he heard the news.

"So. Finally. Chatsworth assumes the black cap. This is the end. The criminals are dragged into court to hear the death sentence. Never mind. Good-bye, Dorothy, my darling. Come, my child. We shall march to the guillotine together."

In those days Imperial Bulldog was still down in Fulham. (They didn't move out to the suburbs until the summer of 1935.) It was quite a long taxi ride. Bergmann's spirits rose as we drove along.

"You have never been inside a film studio before?"

"Only once. Years ago."

"It will interest you, as a phenomenon. You see, the film studio of today is really the palace of the sixteenth century. There one sees what Shakespeare saw: the absolute power of the tyrant, the courtiers, the flatterers, the jesters, the cunningly ambitious intriguers. There are fantastically beautiful women, there are incompetent favorites. There are great men who are suddenly disgraced. There is the most insane extravagance, and unexpected parsimony over a few pence. There is enormous splendor, which is a sham; and also horrible squalor hidden behind the scenery. There are vast schemes, abandoned because of some caprice. There are secrets which everybody knows and no one speaks of. There are even two or three honest advisers. These are the court fools, who speak the deepest wisdom in puns, lest they should be taken seriously. They grimace, and tear their hair privately, and weep."

"You make it sound great fun."

"It is unspeakable," said Bergmann, with relish. "But to us all this does not matter. We have honorably done our task. Now, like Socrates, we pay the penalty of those who tell the truth. We are thrown to the Bulldog to be devoured, and the Umbrella will weep a crocodile tear over our graves."

The outside of the studio was as uninteresting as any modern office building: a big frontage of concrete and glass. Bergmann strode up the steps to the swinging door with such impetus that I couldn't follow him until it had stopped whirling around. He scowled, breathing ferociously, while the doorman took our

names, and a clerk telephoned to announce our
arrival. I caught his eye and grinned, but he
wouldn't smile back. He was obviously plan-
ning his final speech for the defense. I had no
doubt that it would be a masterpiece.

Chatsworth confronted us, as we entered,
across a big desk. The first things I saw were
the soles of his shoes and the smoke of his
cigar. The shoes stood upright on their heels,
elegantly brown and shiny, like a pair of orna-
ments, next to two bronze horses which were
rubbing necks over an inkstand. Sitting apart
from him, but still more or less behind the desk,
were Ashmeade and a very fat man I didn't
know. Our chairs were ready for us, facing
them, isolated in the middle of the room. It
really looked like a tribunal. I drew nearer to
Bergmann, defensively.

"Hullo, you two!" Chatsworth greeted us,
very genial. His head was tilted sideways, holding a telephone against his jaw, like a violin.
"Be with you in a moment." He spoke into the
phone. "Sorry, Dave. Nothing doing. No. I've
made up my mind. . . . Well, he may have told
you that last week. I hadn't seen it then. It
stinks. . . . My dear fellow, I can't help that. I
didn't know they'd do such a rotten job. It's
bloody awful. . . . Well, tell them anything you

like. . . . I don't care if their feelings *are* hurt.
They damn well ought to be hurt. . . . No.
Good-bye."

Ashmeade was smiling subtly. The fat man
looked bored. Chatsworth took his feet off the
desk. His big face came up into view.

"I've got some bad news for you," he told us.

I glanced quickly across at Bergmann; but he
was watching Chatsworth with the glare of a
hypnotist.

"We've just changed our schedule. You'll
have to start shooting in two weeks."

"Impossible!" Bergmann discharged the word
like a gun.

"Of course it's impossible," said Chatsworth,
grinning. "We're impossible people around
here. . . . I don't think you know Mr. Harris? He
sat up all last night doing designs for your sets.
I hope you'll dislike them as much as I
do. . . . Oh, another thing: we can't get Rosemary Lee. She's sailing for New York tomorrow. So I talked to Anita Hayden, and she's
interested. She's a bitch, but she can sing. In a
minute, I want you to come and listen to
Pfeffer's arrangement of the score. It's as noisy
as hell. I don't mind it, though. . . . I've put
Watts on to the lighting. He's our best man. He
knows how to catch the mood."

Bergmann grunted dubiously. I smiled. I liked Chatsworth that morning.

"What about the script?" I asked.

"Don't you worry about that, my lad. Never let a script stand in our way, do we, Sandy? Matter of fact, I can lick that ending of yours. Thought about it this morning, while I was shaving. I have a great idea."

Chatsworth paused to relight his cigar.

"I want you to stay with us," he told me, "right through the picture. Just keep your ears and eyes open. Watch the details. Listen for the intonations. You can help a lot. Bergmann isn't used to the language. Besides, there may be rewrites.... From now on, I'm giving you two an office here in the building, so I'll have my eye on you. If you want anything, just call me. You'll get all the co-operation you need.... Well, I think that takes care of everything. Come along, Doctor. Sandy, will you show Isherwood his new dungeon?"

Thus, as the result of ten minutes' conversation, the whole rhythm of our lives was abruptly changed. For Bergmann, of course, this was nothing new. But I felt dazed. It was as though two hermits had been transported from their cave in the mountains into the middle of a modern railway station. There was no privacy any more. The process of wasting time, which hitherto had been orientally calm and philosphical, now became guilty and apprehensive.

Our "dungeon" was a tiny room on the third floor, forlornly bare, with nothing in it but a desk, three chairs and a telephone. The telephone had a very loud bell. When it rang, we both jumped. The window commanded a view of sooty roofs and the gray winter sky. Outside, along the passage, people went back and forth, making what seemed a deliberately unnecessary amount of noise. Often, their bodies bumped against the door; or it opened, and a head was thrust in. "Where's Joe?" a stranger would ask, somewhat reproachfully. Or else he would say, "Oh, sorry..." and vanish without explanation. These interruptions made Bergmann desperate. "It is the third degree," he would groan. "They torture us, and we have nothing to confess."

We were seldom together for long. The telephone, or a messenger, would summon Bergmann away to confer with Chatsworth, or the casting director, or Mr. Harris, and I would be left with an unfinished scene and his pessimistic advice "to try and think of something." Usually, I didn't even try. I stared out of the window, or gossiped with Dorothy. We had a tacit understanding that, if anybody looked in, we would immediately pretend to be working. Sometimes Dorothy herself left me. She had plenty of friends in the studio, and would slip away for a chat when the coast seemed clear.

Nevertheless, under the pressure of this crisis, we advanced. Bergmann was reckless, now. He was ready to pass even the weakest of my suggestions with little more than a sigh. Also, I myself was getting bolder. My conscience no longer bothered me. The dyer's hand was subdued. There were days when I could write page after page with magical facility. It was really quite easy. Toni joked. The Baron made a pun. Toni's father clowned. Some inner inhibition had been removed. This was simply a job. I was doing it as well as I could.

In the meanwhile, whenever I got a chance, I went exploring. Imperial Bulldog had what was probably the oldest studio site in London. It dated back to early silent days, when directors yelled through megaphones to make themselves heard above the carpenters' hammering; and great flocks of dazed, deafened, limping, hungry extras were driven hither and thither by

aggressive young assistant directors, who
barked at them like sheep dogs. At the time of
the panic, when Sound first came to England
and nobody's job was safe, Bulldog had carried
through a hasty and rather hysterical reconstruction program. The whole place was torn
down and rebuilt at top speed, most of it as
cheaply as possible. No one knew what was
coming next: Taste, perhaps, or Smell, or Stere-
oscopy, or some device that climbed right
down out of the screen and ran around in the
audience. Nothing seemed impossible. And, in
the interim, it was unwise to spend much money on equipment which might be obsolete within a year.

The result of the rebuilding was a maze
of crooked stairways, claustrophobic passages,
abrupt dangerous ramps and Alice-in-Wonder-
land doors. Most of the smaller rooms were
overcrowded, underventilated, separated only by
plywood partitions and lit by naked bulbs hanging from wires. Everything was provisional,
and liable to electrocute you, fall on your head,
or come apart in your hand. "Our motto," said
Lawrence Dwight, "is: 'If it breaks, it's Bulldog.'"

Lawrence was the head cutter on our picture: a short, muscular, angry-looking young

man of about my own age, whose face wore a frown of permanent disgust. We had made friends, chiefly because he had read a story of mine in a magazine, and growled crossly that he liked it. He limped so slightly that I might never have noticed; but, after a few minutes' conversation, he told me abruptly that he had an artificial leg. This he referred to as "my stump." The amputation had followed a motor accident, in which his wife had been killed a month after their marriage.

"We'd just had time to find out that we couldn't stand each other," he told me, angrily watching my face to see if I would be shocked. "I was driving. I suppose I really wanted to murder her."

"I don't know what the hell you imagine you're doing here," he said, a little later. "Selling your soul, I suppose? All you writers have such a bloody romantic attitude. You think you're too good for the movies. Don't you believe it. The movies are too good for you. We don't need any romantic nineteenth-century whores. We need technicians. Thank God, I'm a cutter. I know my job. As a matter of fact, I'm damned good at it. I don't treat film as if it were a bit of my intestine. It's all Chatsworth's fault. He's a romantic, too. He will hire people

like you. Thinks he's Lorenzo the Magnificent
. . . I bet you despise mathematics? Well, let
me tell you something. The movies aren't drama, they aren't literature—they're pure mathematics. Of course, you'll never understand that,
as long as you live."

Lawrence took great pleasure in pointing out
to me the many inefficiencies of the studio. For
instance, there was no proper storage room for
scenery. Sets had to be broken up as soon as
they had been used; the waste of materials was
appalling. And then, Bulldog carried so many
passengers. "We could do a much better job
with two-thirds of our present staff. All these
assistant directors, fussing about and falling
over each other . . . They even have what they
call dialogue directors. Can you imagine? Some
poor stooge who sits around on his fat behind
and says 'Yes' whenever anybody looks at
him."

I laughed. "That's what I'm going to do."

But Lawrence wasn't in the least embarrassed. "I might have known it," he said dis-
gustedly. "You're just the right type. So bloody
tactful."

His deepest scorn was reserved for the Reading Department, officially known as Annex G.
The back lot of Imperial Bulldog sloped down

to the river. Annex G had originally been a
warehouse. It reminded me of a lawyer's office
in a Dickens novel. There were cobwebbed
shelves, rows and rows of them, right up to the
roof; and not a crack anywhere wide enough to
insert your little finger. The lower rows were
mostly scripts; scripts in duplicate and tripli-
cate, treatments, rough drafts, every scrap of
paper on which any Bulldog writer had ever
scribbled. Lawrence told me that the rats had
gnawed long tunnels through them, from end
to end. "They ought to be dumped in the
Thames," Lawrence added, "but the River Police would prosecute us for poisoning the
water."

And then there were books. These were the
novels and plays which the studio had bought
to make into pictures. At any rate, that was
what they were supposed to be. Had Bulldog
ever considered filming *Bradshaw's Railway
Timetable for 1911?* Well, perhaps that had
come originally from the Research Department. "But will you explain to me," said
Lawrence, "why we have twenty-seven copies
of *Half Hours with a Microscope,* one of them
stolen from the Woking Public Library?"

Rather to my surprise, Lawrence approved of
Bergmann and admired him. He had seen

several of the pictures Bergmann had directed in Germany; and this, of course, delighted Bergmann, although he would never admit it. Instead, he praised Lawrence's character, calling him *"ein anstaendiger Junge."* Whenever they met, Bergmann addressed him as "Master." After a while, Lawrence started to reciprocate. Whereupon Bergmann, never to be outdone, began to call Lawrence "Grand Master." Lawrence took to calling me "Herr Talk-Director." I called him "Herr Cut-Master."

I was careful, however, not to inform Bergmann of Lawrence's political opinions. "All of this fascist-communist nonsense," said Lawrence, "is so bloody old-fashioned. People rave about the workers. It makes me sick. The workers are just sheep. Always have been. Always will be. They choose to be that way, and why shouldn't they? It's their life. And they dodge a lot of headaches. . . . Take the men at this place. What do they know or care about anything, except getting their pay checks? If any problem arises outside their immediate job, they expect someone else to decide it for them. Quite right, too, from their point of view. A country has to be run by a minority of some sort. The only thing is, we've got to get rid of these damned sentimental politicians. All politicians are amateurs. It's as if we'd handed over the studio to the Publicity Department. The only people who really matter are the technicians. They know what they want."

"And what do they want?"

"They want efficiency."

"What's that?"

"Efficiency is doing a job for the sake of doing a job."

"But why should you do a job, anyway? What's the incentive?"

"The incentive is to fight anarchy. That's all Man lives for. Reclaiming life from its natural muddle. Making patterns."

"Patterns for what?"

"For the sake of patterns. To create meaning. What else is there?"

"And what about the things that won't fit into your patterns?"

"Discard them."

"You mean, kill Jews?"

"Don't try to shock me with your bloody sentimental false analogies. You know perfectly well what I mean. When people refuse to fit into patterns, they discard themselves. That's not my fault. Hitler doesn't make patterns. He's just an opportunist. When you make patterns, you don't persecute. Patterns aren't people."

"Who's being old-fasioned now? That sounds like Art for Art's sake."

"I don't care what it sounds like. . . . Technicians are the only real artists, anyway."

"It's all very well for you to make patterns with your cutting. But what's the use, when you have to work on pictures like *Prater Violet*?"

"That's Chatsworth's worry, and Bergmann's, and yours. If you so-called artists would behave like technicians and get together, and stop playing at being democrats, you'd make the public take the kind of picture you wanted. This business about the box office is just a sentimental democratic fiction. If you stuck together and refused to make anything but, say, abstract films, the public would have to go and see them, and like them. . . . Still, it's no use talking. You'll never have the guts. You'd much rather whine about prostitution, and keep on making *Prater Violets*. And that's why the public despises you, in its heart. It knows damn well it's got you by the short hairs. . . . Only, one thing: don't come to me with your artistic sorrows, because I'm not interested."

We started shooting the picture in the final

week of January. I give this approximate date because it is almost the last I shall be able to remember. What followed is so confused in my memory, so transposed and foreshortened, that I can only describe it synthetically. My recollection of it has no sequence. It is all of a piece.

Within the great barnlike sound-stage, with its high bare padded walls, big enough to enclose an airship, there is neither day nor night: only irregular alternations of activity and silence. Beneath a firmament of girders and catwalks, out of which the cowled lamps shine coldly down like planets, stands the inconsequent, half-dismantled architecture of the sets; archways, sections of houses, wood and canvas hills, huge photographic backdrops, the frontages of streets; a kind of Pompeii, but more desolate, more uncanny, because this is, literally, a half-world, a limbo of mirror-images, a town which has lost its third dimension. Only the tangle of heavy power cables is solid, and apt to trip you as you cross the floor. Your footsteps sound unnaturally loud; you find yourself walking on tiptoe.

In one corner, amidst these ruins, there is life. A single set is brilliantly illuminated. From the distance, it looks like a shrine, and the figures standing around it might be worshippers. But it is merely the living room of Toni's home, complete with period furniture, gaily colored curtains, a canary cage and a cuckoo clock. The men who are putting the finishing touches to this charming, life-size doll's house go about their work with the same matter-of-fact, unsmiling efficiency which any carpenters and electricians might show in building a garage.

In the middle of the set, patient and anonymous as tailors' dummies, are the actor and actress who are standing in for Arthur Cromwell and Anita Hayden. Mr. Watts, a thin bald man with gold-rimmed spectacles, walks restlessly back and forth, regarding them from various angles. A blue-grass monocle hangs from a ribbon around his neck. He raises it repeatedly to observe the general effect of the lighting; and the gesture is incongruously like that of a Regency fop. Beside him is Fred Murray, red-haired and wearing rubber shoes. Fred is what is called 'the Gaffer," in studio slang. According to our etiquette, Mr. Watts cannot condescend to give orders directly. He murmurs them to Fred; and Fred, as if translating into a foreign language, shouts up to the men who work the lamps on the catwalk, high above.

"Put a silk on that rifle.... Take a couple of turns on number four. . . . Kill that baby."

"I'm ready," says Mr. Watts, at length.

"All right," Fred Murray shouts to his assistants. "Save them." The arcs are switched off and the house lights go on. The set loses its shrinelike glamour. The stand-ins leave their positions. There is an atmosphere of anticlimax, as though we were about to start all over again from the beginning.

"Now then, are we nearly ready?" This is Eliot, the assistant director. He has a long pointed nose and a public-school accent. He carries a copy of the script, like an emblem of office, in his hand. His manner is bossy, but self-conscious and unsure. I feel sorry for him. His job makes him unpopular. He has to fuss and keep things moving; and he doesn't know how to do it without being aggressive. He doesn't know how to talk to the older men, or the stagehands. He is conscious of his own high-pitched, cultured voice. His shirt collar has too much starch in it.

"What's the hold-up?" Eliot plaintively addresses the world in general. "What about you, Roger?"

Roger, the sound-recordist, curses under his breath. He hates being rushed. "There's a baffle on this mike," he explains, with acid patience. "It's a bloody lively set. . . . Shift your boom a bit more round to the left, Teddy. We'll have to use a flower pot."

The boom moves over, dangling the microphone, like a fishing rod. Teddy, who works it, crosses the set and conceals a second microphone behind a china figure on the table.

Meanwhile, somewhere in the background, I hear Arthur Cromwell calling, "Where's the invaluable Isherwood?" Arthur plays Toni's father. He is a big handsome man who used to be a matinee idol—a real fine old ham. He wants me to hear him do his part. When he forgets a line, he snaps his fingers, without impatience.

"What's the matter, Toni? Isn't it time to go to the Prater?"

"Aren't you going to the Prater today?" I prompt.

"Aren't you going to the Prater today?" But Arthur has some mysterious actor's inhibition about this. "Bit of a mouthful, isn't it? I can't hear myself saying that, somehow. . . . How about 'Why aren't you at the Prater?' "

"All right."

Bergmann calls, "Isherwood!" (Since we have been working in the studio, he always addresses me by my surname in public.) He

marches away from the set with his hands
behind his back, not even glancing around to
see if I am following. We go through the dou-
ble doors and out onto the fire-escape. Everybody retires to the fire-escape when they want
to talk and smoke, because smoking isn't allowed inside the building. I nod to the doorman, who is reading the *Daily Herald* through
his pince-nez. He is a great admirer of Soviet
Russia.

Standing on the little iron platform, we can
see a glimpse of the chilly gray river beyond
the rooftops. The air smells damp and fresh,
after being indoors, and there is a breeze which
ruffles Bergmann's bushy hair.

"How is the scene? Is it all right like this?"

"Yes, I think so." I try to sound convincing. I
feel lazy, this morning, and don't want any
trouble. We both examine our copies of the
script; or, at least, I pretend to. I have read it so
often that the words have lost their meaning.

Bergmann frowns and grunts. "I thought,
maybe, if we could find something. It seems so
bare, so poor. . . . Couldn't perhaps Toni say, 'I
cannot sell the violets of yesterday; they are
unfresh?' "

" 'I can't sell yesterday's violets; they wither
so quickly.' "

95

"Good. Good . . . Write that down."

I write it into the script. Eliot appears at the door. "Ready to rehearse now, sir."

"Let us go." Bergmann leads the way back to the set, with Eliot and myself following—a general attended by his staff. Everybody watches us, wondering if anything important has been decided. There is a childish satisfaction in having kept so many people waiting.

Eliot goes over to the door of Anita Hayden's portable dressing room. "Miss Hayden," he says, very self-consciously, "would you come now, please? We're ready."

Anita, looking like a petulant little girl in her short flowered dress, apron and frilly petticoats, emerges and walks onto the set. Like nearly all famous people, she seems a size smaller than her photographs.

I approach her, afraid that this is going to be unpleasant. I try to grin. "Sorry! We've changed a line again."

But Anita, for some reason, is in a good mood.

"Brute!" she exclaims, coquettishly. "Well, come on, let's hear the worst."

Eliot blows his whistle. "Quiet there! Dead quiet! Full rehearsal! Green light!" This last order is for the doorman, who will switch on the sign over the sound-stage door: "Rehearsal. Enter quietly."

At last we are ready. The rehearsal begins.

Toni is standing alone, looking pensively out of the window. It is the day after her meeting with Rudolf. And now she has just received a letter of love and farewell, cryptically worded, because he cannot tell her the whole truth: that he is the Prince and that he has been summoned to Borodania. So Toni is heartbroken and bewildered. Her eyes are full of tears. (This part of the scene is covered by a close-up.)

The door opens. Toni's father comes in.

Father: "What's the matter, Toni? Why aren't you at the Prater?"

Toni (inventing an excuse): "I—I haven't any flowers."

Father: "Did you sell all you had yesterday?"

Toni (with a faraway look in her eyes, which shows that her answer is symbolic): "I can't sell yesterday's violets. They wither so quickly."

She begins to sob, and runs out of the room, banging the door. Her father stands looking after her, in blank surprise. Then he shrugs his shoulders and grimaces, as much as to say that woman's whims are beyond his understanding.

"Cut." Bergmann rises quickly from his chair and goes over to Anita. "Let me tell you something, Madame. The way you throw open that door is great. It is altogether much too great. You give to the movement a theatrical importance beside which the slaughter of Rasputin is just a quick breakfast."

Anita smiles graciously. "Sorry, Friedrich. I *felt* it wasn't right." She *is* in a good mood.

"Let me show you, once..." Bergmann stands by the table. His lips tremble, his eyes glisten; he is a beautiful young girl on the verge of tears. "I cannot sell violets of yesterday ... They wither..." He runs, with face averted, from the room. There is a bump, behind the scenes, and a muttered, "*Verflucht!*" He must have tripped over one of the cables. An instant later, Bergmann reappears, grinning, a little out of breath. "You see how I mean? With a certain lightness. Do not hit it too hard."

"Yes," Anita nods seriously, playing up to him. "I *think* I see."

"All right, my darling," Bergmann pats her arm. "We shoot it once."

"Where's Timmy?" Anita demands, in a bored, melodious voice. The make-up man hurries forward. "Timmy darling, is my face all right?"

She submits it to him, as impersonally as one extends a shoe to the bootblack; this anxiously pretty mask which is her job, her source of income, the tool of her trade. Timmy dabs at it expertly. She glances at herself coldly, without vanity, in his pocket mirror. The camera operator's assistant measures the distance from the lens to her nose, with a tape.

A boy named George asks the continuity girl for the number of the scene. It has to be chalked on the board which he will hold in front of the camera, before the take.

Roger calls from the sound booth, "Come in for this one, Chris. I need an alibi." He often says this, jokingly, but with a certain veiled resentment, which is directed chiefly against Eliot. Roger resents any criticism of the sound recording. He is very conscientious about his job.

I go into the sound booth, which is like a telephone box. Eliot begins to shout bossily, "Right! Ready, sir? Ready, Mr. Watts? Bell, please. Doors! Red light!" Then, because some people are still moving about, "Quiet! This is a take!"

Roger picks up the headphones and plugs in

to the sound-camera room, which is in a gallery, overlooking the floor. "Ready to go, Jack?" he asks. Two buzzes: the okay signal.

"Are we all set?" asks Eliot. Then, after a moment, "Turn them over."

"Running," the boy at the switchboard tells him.

George steps forward and holds the board up before the camera.

Roger buzzes twice to the sound camera. Two buzzes in reply. Roger buzzes twice to signal Bergmann that Sound is ready.

Clark, the boy who works the clappers, says in a loud voice, "104, take one." He claps the clappers.

Bergmann, sitting grim in his chair, hisses between shut teeth, "Camera!"

I watch him, throughout the take. It isn't necessary to look at the set; the whole scene is reflected in his face. He never shifts his eyes from the actors for an instant. He seems to control every gesture, every intonation, by a sheer effort of hypnotic power. His lips move, his face relaxes and contracts, his body is thrust forward or drawn back in its seat, his hands rise and fall to mark the phases of the action. Now he is coaxing Toni from the window, now warning against too much haste, now encouraging her father, now calling for more expression, now afraid the pause will be missed, now delighted with the tempo, now anxious again, now really alarmed, now reassured, now touched, now pleased, now very pleased, now cautious, now disturbed, now amused. Bergmann's concentration is marvelous in its singleness of purpose. It is the act of creation.

When it is all over, he sighs, as if awaking from sleep. Softly, lovingly, he breathes the word, "Cut."

He turns to the camera operator. "How was it?"

"All right, sir, but I'd like to go again."

Roger gives two buzzes.

"Okay for sound, sir," says Teddy.

Joyce, the continuity girl, checks the footage with the operator. Roger puts his head out of the booth. "Teddy, will you favor round toward Miss Hayden a bit? I'm afraid of that bloody camera."

This problem of camera noise is perpetual. To guard against it, the camera is muffled in a quilt, which makes it look like a pet poodle wearing its winter jacket. Nevertheless, the noise persists. Bergmann never fails to react to it. Sometimes he curses, sometimes he sulks. This morning, however, he is in a clowning mood. He goes over to the camera and throws his arms around it.

"My dear old friend, we make you work so hard! It's too cruel! Mr. Chatsworth should give you a pension, and send you to the meadow to eat grass with the retired racehorses."

Everybody laughs. Bergmann is quite popular on the floor. "He's what I call a regular comedian," the doorman tells me. "This picture will be good, if it's half as funny as he is."

Mr. Watts and the camera operator are discussing how to avoid the mike shadow. Bergmann calls it "the Original Sin of the Talking Pictures." On rare occasions, the microphone itself somehow manages to get into the shot, without anybody noticing it. There is something sinister about it, like Poe's Raven. It is always there, silently listening.

A long buzz from the sound-camera room. Roger puts on the headphones and reports, "Sound camera reloading, sir." Bergmann gives a grunt and goes off into a corner to dictate a poem to Dorothy. Amidst all this turmoil, he still finds time to compose one, nearly every day. Fred Murray is shouting directions for the readjustment of various lamps on the spot-rail and gantry; the tweets, the snooks and the baby spots. Joyce is typing the continuity report, which contains the exact text of each scene, as acted, with details of footage, screentime, hours of work and so forth.

"Come on," shouts Eliot. "Aren't we ready, yet?"

Roger calls up to the camera room, "Going again, Jack."

Teddy notices that Eliot is inadvertently standing in front of Roger's window, blocking our view of the set. He grins maliciously, and says, in an obvious parody of Eliot's most officious tone, "Clear the booth, please!" Eliot blushes and moves aside, murmuring, "Sorry." Roger winks at me. Teddy, very pleased with himself, swings the microphone-boom over, whistling, and warning his crew, "Mind your heads, my braves!"

Roger generally lets me ring the bell for silence and make the two-buzz signal. It is one of the few opportunities I get of earning my salary. But, this time, I am mooning. I watch Bergmann telling something funny to Fred Murray, and wonder what it is. Roger has to make the signals himself. "I'm sorry to see a falling off in your wonted efficiency, Chris," he tells me. And he adds, to Teddy, "I was thinking of giving Chris his ticket, but now I shall have to reconsider it."

Roger's nautical expressions date back to the
time when he was a radio operator on a mer-
chant ship. He still has something of the ship's
officer about him, in his brisk movements, his
conscientiousness, his alert, pink, open-air face.
He studies yachting magazines in the booth,
between takes.

"Quiet! Get settled down. Ready? Turn them
over."

"Running."

"104, take two."

"Camera . . ."

"Cut."

"Okay, sir."

"Okay for sound, Mr. Bergmann."

"All right. We print this one."

"Are you going again, sir?"

"We shoot it once more, quickly."

"Right. Come on, now. Let's get in the can."

But the third take is N.G. Anita fluffs a line.
In the middle of the fourth take, the camera
jams. The fifth take is all right, and will be
printed. My long, idle, tiring morning is over,
and it is time for lunch.

There was a choice of three places to eat.
Imperial Bulldog had its own canteen on the
premises; but this was so crowded with studio

workers, secretaries, bit players and extras that you could hardly ever find room to sit down. Then there was a public house, right across the street, where the food was quite good. This was the resort of the intellectuals: the writers, the cutters, the musicians and the members of the Art Department. I always tried to persuade Bergmann to go there; for we invariably had our meals together. But he usually insisted on the third alternative, a big hotel in South Kensington, where the studio executives and directors ate. Bergmann went to the hotel on principle. "One has to show one's self," he told me. "The animals expect to see their trainer." He had a half-humorous, half-serious theory that the powers of Bulldog were eternally plotting against him, and that, if he didn't put in an appearance, they would somehow contrive to liquidate him altogether.

The hotel had an imposing dining room and bad, would-be Continental food. Bergmann would enter it in his grimmest, most majestic mood, his eyebrows drawn down formidably, shooting severe glances to left and right. Catching the eyes of his colleagues, he would bow stiffly, but seldom speak. We had a small table to ourselves; unless, as sometimes happened, we were invited to sit with one of the Bulldog groups.

My chief objection to the hotel, apart from its boredom, was the expense. Earning so much money had made me curiously stingy, and I grudged spending it on food. So I began to eat less and less, saying that I wasn't hungry. By ordering only a plate of soup or a sweet I managed to cut my bill down to about two shillings a day.

Neither Bergmann nor any of the others seemed to find this remarkable. Many of them had bad digestions, due to their sedentary occupation, and were on a diet. But there was a little waiter who, for some reason, had taken a fancy to me. We always exchanged a few words when I came in. One day, when I was sitting in a large group and had ordered, as usual, the cheapest item on the menu, he came up behind my chair and whispered, "Why not take the Lobster Newburg, sir? The other gentlemen have ordered it. There'll be enough for one extra. I won't charge you anything."

After the bustle of the morning, our afternoon begins in a leisurely, relaxed mood. We have migrated to another sound-stage, where a new set has been built: Toni's bedroom. The first scene to be shot is the one immediately preceding the arrival of Rudolf's letter. Toni is lying in bed, asleep, a smile on her lips. She is dreaming of her lover and yesterday's romantic meeting. Outside, it is a brilliant spring morning. Toni stirs, wakes, stretches herself, jumps out of bed, runs across the room, throws open the window, breathes in the perfume of the flowers delightedly, and bursts into the theme song of the picture.

We can hear Anita practicing it now, with Pfeffer at the piano, somewhere behind the set:

> Spring wakes,
> Winter's dead.
> Ice breaks,
> Frosts have fled.
> Mornings are blue as your eyes,
> And from the skies
> I hear a lark
> Sing . . .

Anita breaks off, abruptly, "Damn, I missed that beat again. Sorry, darling. Let's try it once more."

> Spring wakes,
> Winter's dead.

> Ice breaks,
> Frosts have fled ...

Meanwhile, the carpenters, with a magnificent disregard for Art, are hammering and chiseling away at the bedroom windowsill. But George, the romantic, hums the tune and smiles dreamily as he writes on his board. George is an Irish boy, dark, good-looking, and full of innocent conceit. He flirts with Dorothy, Joyce and any attractive extras who come around the set. No doubt his fantasy even aspires to Anita herself. Joyce likes him; Dorothy is not impressed. "Kids of his age are more trouble than they're worth," she tells me. "I like a man to be sophisticated, if you know what I mean."

> Last year's
> Flowers were gay,
> But who cares
> For yesterday?

George strolls over to Roger, Teddy and myself, grinning and humming. When Anita gets to the refrain, he joins in, so that they sing a kind of long-distance duet:

> Flowers must fade, and yet

One I can't forget:
Prater Vi-o-let.

Roger and Teddy clap their hands ironically.
George bows, complacently taking the ap-
plause for what it is worth, and a bit extra.

"You know," he confides to us, with his art-
less smile, "I like that old-fashioned stuff. It
gets me."

"How's the Great Lover today?" Teddy asks
him. "And who's that little piece of goods I saw
you with in the canteen?"

George smirks, "Just a friend of mine."

"She looked young enough to be your grand-
daughter, you nasty old man."

"Our nurseries are no longer safe," says Roger. "I shall have to clean the family blunder-
buss. . . . Which reminds me, Teddy, my boy:
when are we going to hear those wedding
bells?"

Teddy blushes, and becomes serious at once.
His engagement, to a girl in the Art Department, is a standard topic of studio humor.

"As a matter of fact," he tells us gravely,
"Mary and I had a talk about it last night.
We've agreed to wait a while. I want to work
up a better job. In five years . . ."

"Five years!" I am really shocked. "But Teddy, anything may happen in five years. Suppose there's a war?"

"All the same," says Teddy stolidly, "a chap's got to be able to offer his wife a proper home."

Teddy is like that. No doubt he really will wait, if Mary lets him. He is a steady boy, solid all through. I can see him at forty, at fifty, at sixty, still just the same. He saves his money, and plays rugger on Saturday afternoons. Once a week, he and Fred Murray go to watch the All-In Wrestling at the local baths. They are both ardent fans, and spend a lot of time arguing about the merits of their respective favorites, Norman the Butcher and the Golden Hawk.

> Flowers must fade, and yet
> One I can't forget:
> Prater Vi-o-let.

The carpenters are still working on the window. Bergmann is still downstairs in the projection room, looking at the rushes: the prints of the film that was shot yesterday. Probably we shan't get started for another hour, at least. I wander off by myself to see what is happening on the other stages.

On Stage One, they are building our big

restaurant set. This is for the final sequence of the picture. It is here, according to Chatsworth's revised version, that Toni takes her revenge on Rudolf by pretending to be the mistress of the notorious Baron Goldschrank. The Baron, an old admirer, can refuse her nothing, and rather unwillingly agrees to help in the plot. Toni makes a sensational entrance, on his arm, at the top of the staircase, in a blaze of borrowed diamonds. Rudolf, who is present, springs to his feet and strikes the Baron across the mouth. A duel is arranged, there and then, despite the Baron's timidity and Toni's attempted explanations. The Baron, as the injured party, is about to take the first shot, and Rudolf is striking an heroic attitude, when Count Rosanoff rushes in and throws himself between them, exclaiming, "Kill me, but do not dare to harm His Royal Highness!" For the wicked uncle has been overthrown, the King knows all and sends his blessing, and the way is open for Rudolf's return to Borodania with Toni as his bride.

Well, at any rate, the music is quite pretty.

On Stage Three, Eddie Kennedy is directing *Ten's a Honeymoon*. He is a dynamic, red-faced man, with bulging eyes and a wheezy voice, who specializes in American-style farces, full of mugging and slick lines. Having spent a year in Hollywood, he is regarded as an expert. And he certainly dresses the part. He is in his shirt-sleeves, with his hat on, and a chewed cigar sticking out of the corner of his big mouth. He calls his actors "laddie" and his actresses "baby" or "sugar." He works very fast, with immense decision, shouting, swearing, bullying and keeping everybody in a good humor. I stand there a long time, watching the comedian's efforts to rescue a fat lady from a portable Turkish bath. The assistant director tells me proudly that the picture will be finished by the end of this week, five days ahead of schedule.

I come back to our set, to find Bergmann returned and Anita already in bed, under a battery of lights, waiting for a close-up. Roger is talking to Timmy, the make-up man, and Clark.

"Hullo, Chris," Roger greets me. "Anita was asking for you."

"She was?"

"Said she wanted you to get in there and keep her warm. She's lonely."

"Why didn't one of you gentlemen oblige?"

"I wouldn't mind," says Clark. He means it. He is a tall skinny boy with a ferret's eyes and an unpleasantly small mouth.

"She's married, isn't she?" Roger asks.

"Used to be," says Timmy, "to Oliver Gilchrist. They got divorced."

"I don't blame him. She'd be a devil to live with. I know her sort," Roger mimics. " 'Not now, darling. I've got *such* a headache, and my hair's been waved.' And she tells her girl friends, 'Men all want the same thing. They're such *brutes.*' "

Timmy rolls his eyes, and sings, sotto voce:

> Just the same, I'll bet
> You're not hard to get:
> Prater Vi-o-let.

"Now then, everybody ready?" shouts Eliot, eyeing us with disapproval. "Let's get started."

We scatter to our respective positions.

The close-up takes nearly two hours. Watts fusses endlessly over the lighting. The camera jams. Anita begins to sulk. Arthur Cromwell is getting peevish. He has an appointment. Why couldn't they have shot his scene first? (It belongs to the last sequence, when Toni's father comes home late and finds she hasn't returned.) "I think I'm entitled to some consideration," he tells me, plaintively. "After all, I've been a star for fifteen years."

In the middle of this, Ashmeade pays us a visit, with Mr. Harris. They have heard of a place in Essex where it might be possible to shoot some exteriors for the Prater scenes. Wouldn't Bergmann care to go down with Harris next weekend and look at it?

But Bergmann is firm. He smiles his blandest, most subtle smile. "A Sunday without Harris is my religion."

Harris can't very well take offense at this, so he and Ashmeade have to force a laugh; but they aren't pleased. Bergmann dislikes Harris, and Harris knows it. (In private, Bergmann calls him "the art-constrictor.") Ashmeade and Harris retire, baffled.

At five o'clock, the word goes round that we shall be working late. The union men get paid overtime, but they grumble, like the rest of us. Clark is particularly bitter; this is the third date he's had to break with his girl. "Eddie Kennedy's unit," he complains, "hasn't worked late since the picture started. What we need is more organization." Teddy, who is very loyal to Bergmann, feels that this is going too far. "Slapstick's different," he points out. "You can't rush this high-class stuff. It's got to be artistic."

I go to the telephone and dial my home number.

"Hullo."

"Oh, Christopher . . . Does this mean you won't be into supper again?"

"I'm afraid so."

"And we're having fishcakes!"

After the close-up, there is a tracking-shot, which will take time to prepare. The dolly, on which the camera will retreat before Toni's advance to the bedroom window, is apt to emit loud squeaks, audible to the microphone. It has to be oiled and tested. Roger and I go out to the fire-escape for a smoke. It is quite dark now, but not cold. The electric Bulldog sign casts a red light on the angle of the building.

Roger is feeling depressed.

"I don't know why I hang on to this job," he tells me. "The pay's all right. But it doesn't lead anywhere. . . . Next month, I'll be thirty-four. Know how I spend my evenings, Chris? Designing a boat. I've got it all figured out, even down to the cabin fixtures. It wouldn't cost much to build, either. I've saved a bit."

"What would you do with it?"

"Just sail away."

"Well, why don't you?"

"I don't know. . . . Places are all the same, really. I've been around."

"Haven't you ever thought of getting married?"

"Oh, I tried that, too. When I was a kid . . . She died."

"I'm sorry."

"It wasn't so ruddy wonderful. She was a good girl, though. . . . You know, sometimes I wonder what all this is for. Why not just peacefully end it?"

"We all think that. But we don't do it."

"Surely you're not fool enough to imagine there's anything afterwards?"

"Perhaps. No, I suppose not . . . I don't think it makes much difference."

Now that we have touched rock-bottom, Roger suddenly brightens. "You know what have been the best things in my life, Chris? Good, unexpected lays."

And he tells me the story of a married woman he once met in a hotel in Burton-on-Trent.

At seven-thirty, a boy from the canteen brings up tea and sandwiches. Eating together like this seems to raise the spirits of the entire unit. Anita has finished her scene, and another close-up, and gone home; she can be very co-operative when it suits her. Arthur Cromwell's scene won't take long. We shall be through by nine, after all.

Lawrence Dwight comes up from the cutting room to watch us.

He is scowling, as usual, but I can see that he feels pleased with himself. He has had a good day.

"Good evening, Herr Cut-Master. How are the patterns?"

"The patterns are a damn sight better than you deserve," says Lawrence, "considering the muck you send us. I'm going to make you quite a nice little picture, for which you'll take all the credit."

"That's ghastly decent of you."

Bergmann is pacing the floor, as he often does just before a take. He comes right up to us and stands for a moment, regarding our faces with dark, troubled, unseeing eyes. Then he turns abruptly and walks away in a kind of trance.

"Come on, now," shouts Eliot. "Let's get going. We don't want to be here all night."

"He's wasting his talents," says Lawrence. "What an ideal nursery governess!"

"Dead quiet, please!"

By ten minutes to nine, it is all over. We have shot two thousand feet of film. The day's work represents four minutes and thirty seconds of the completed picture.

"What are you doing this evening?" Lawrence asks.

"Nothing special. Why?"

"Let's go to a movie."

"Poor Dr. Bergmann," said my mother, when I came down to breakfast one morning, in the middle of February. "I'm afraid he'll be very worried about his family."

"What do you mean?"

"They're still in Vienna, aren't they? It seems dreadfully unsettled there, just now."

I picked up the newspaper. The word "Austria" jumped at me from the headlines. I was too excited to read properly. My eye caught bits of sentences, proper names: "At Linz, after heavy fighting . . . Fey . . . Starhemberg . . . martial law . . . hundreds of arrests . . . general strike fails to . . . Viennese workers besieged . . . hunt out socialist hyenas, Dollfuss declares . . ."

I dropped the paper, ran out into the hall, and dialed Bergmann's number. His voice answered as soon as the bell began to ring. "Hullo, yes . . ."

"Hullo, Friedrich."

"Oh . . . Hullo, Christopher." He sounded

weary and disappointed. Obviously, he had been expecting some other call.

"Friedrich, I've just read the news . . ."

"Yes." His voice had no expression in it at all.

"Is there anything I can do?"

"There is nothing any of us can do, my child."

"Would you like me to come round?"

Bergmann sighed. "Very well. Yes. If you wish."

I hung up and phoned for a taxi. While I was waiting for it, I hastily swallowed some breakfast. My mother and Richard watched me in silence. Bergmann had become part of their lives, although they had only seen him once, for a few minutes, one day when he came to the house to fetch me. This was a family crisis.

Bergmann was sitting in the living room when I arrived, facing the telephone, his head propped in his hands. I was shocked by his appearance. He looked so tired and old.

"*Servus*," he said. He didn't raise his eyes. I saw that he had been crying.

I sat down at his side and put my arm around him. "Friedrich . . . You mustn't worry. They'll be all right."

"I have been trying to speak to them," Bergmann told me, wearily. "But it is impossible. There is no communication. Just now, I sent a telegram. It will be delayed for many hours. For days, perhaps."

"I'm sure they'll be all right. After all, Vienna is a big city. The fighting's localized, the paper says. Probably it won't last long."

Bergmann shook his head. "This is only the beginning. Now, anything may happen. Hitler has his opportunity. In a few hours, there can be war."

"He wouldn't dare. Mussolini would stop him. Didn't you read what the *Times* correspondent in Rome said about . . . ?"

But he wasn't listening to me. His whole body was trembling. He began to sob, helplessly, covering his face with his hands. At length, he gasped out, "I am so afraid . . ."

"Friedrich, don't. Please don't."

After a moment, he recovered a little. He looked up. He rose to his feet, and began to walk about the room. There was a long silence.

"If by this evening I hear nothing," he told me, suddenly, "I must go to them."

"But, Friedrich . . ."

"What else can I do? I have no choice."

"You wouldn't be able to help them."

Bergmann sighed. "You do not understand. How can I leave them alone at such a time?

Already, they have endured so much.... You are very kind, Christopher. You are my only friend in this country. But you cannot understand. You have always been safe and protected. Your home has never been threatened. You cannot know what it is like to be an exile, a perpetual stranger.... I am bitterly ashamed that I am here, in safety."

"But they wouldn't want you to be with them. Don't you realize, they must be glad you're safe? You might even compromise them. After all, lots of people must know about your political opinions. You might be arrested."

Bergmann shrugged his shoulders. "All that is unimportant. You do not understand."

"Besides," I unwisely continued, "they wouldn't want you to leave the picture."

All Bergmann's pent-up anxiety exploded. "The picture! I s—— up the picture! This heartless filth! This wretched, lying charade! To make such a picture at such a moment is definitely heartless. It is a crime. It definitely aids Dollfuss, and Starhemberg, and Fey and all their gangsters. It covers up the dirty syphilitic sore with rose leaves, with the petals of this hypocritical reactionary violet. It lies and declares that the pretty Danube is blue, when the water is red with blood.... I am punished for

assisting at this lie. We shall all be punished...."

The telephone rang. Bergmann seized it
"Yes, hullo. Yes ..." His face darkened. "It is
the studio," he told me. "You speak to them."

"Hullo, Mr. Isherwood?" said the voice of
Chatsworth's secretary, very brightly. "My
word, you're up early this morning! Well, that's
splendid—because Mr. Harris is a little bit worried. He's not sure about some details in the
next set. Perhaps you could come in a little
sooner and talk things over before you start
work?"

I covered the mouthpiece with my hand. "Do
you want me to tell them you're not well?" I
asked Bergmann.

"Moment ... Wait ... No. Do not say that."
He sighed deeply. "We must go."

It was an awful day. Bergmann went
through it in a kind of stupor, and I watched
him anxiously, fearing some outburst. During
the takes, he sat like a dummy, seeming not to
care what happened. If spoken to, he answered
briefly and listlessly. He made no criticisms, no
objection to anything. Unless Roger or the
camera operator said "No," the scene would be
printed; and we went on dully to the next.

Everybody in the unit reacted to his mood.

Anita made difficulties, Cromwell hammed, Eliot fussed idiotically, the electricians were lazy, Mr. Watts wasted hours on lighting. Only Roger and Teddy were efficient, quiet and considerate. I had tried to explain to them how Bergmann was feeling. Teddy's only comment was, "Rotten luck." But he meant it.

In the evening, just as we were finishing work, a telegram arrived from Vienna: "Don't be silly, Friedrich dear. You know how newspapers exaggerate. Inge is still on holiday in the mountains with friends. I have just made a cake. Mother says it is delicious and sends love. Many kisses."

Bergmann showed it to me, smiling, with tears in his eyes. "She is great," he said. "Definitely great."

But now his personal trouble gave way to political anxiety and anger, which grew from day to day. Throughout Tuesday and Wednesday, the struggle continued. Without definite orders, without leadership, cut off and isolated into small groups, the workers went on fighting What else could they do? Their homes, the great modern tenements, admired by the whole of Europe as the first architecture of a new and better world, were now described by the Press as "red fortresses"; and the government artillery was shooting them to pieces. The socialist leaders, fearing this emergency, had provided secret stores of arms and ammunition; but the leaders were all arrested now, or in hiding. Nobody knew where the weapons were buried. Desperately, men dug in courtyards and basements, and found nothing. Dollfuss took tea with the Papal Nuncio. Starhemberg saw forty-two corpses laid out in the captured Goethe Hof, and commented: "Far too few!" Berlin looked on, smugly satisfied. Another of its enemies was being destroyed; and Hitler's hands were clean.

Bergmann listened eagerly to every news broadcast, bought every special edition. During those first two days, while the workers still held out, I knew that he was hoping against hope. Perhaps the street fighting would grow into a revolution. Perhaps international Labor would force the Powers to intervene. There was just one little chance—one in a million. And then there was no chance at all.

Bergmann raged in his despair. He wanted to write letters to the conservative Press, protesting against its studied tone of neutrality. The letters were written, but I had to persuade him not to send them. He had no case. The papers were being perfectly fair, according to their own standards. You couldn't expect anything else.

By the beginning of the next week, it was all over, except for the government's vengeance on its prisoners. The workers' tenements were made to fly the white flag. The Engels Hof was renamed the Dollfuss Hof. Every man over eighteen from the Schlinger Hof was in prison, including the sick and the cripples. Terrorism became economical since a new law stopped the unemployment pay of those who had been arrested. Meanwhile, Frau Dollfuss went among the workers' families, distributing cakes. Dollfuss was sincerely sad: "I hope the blood that flowed in our land will bring people to their senses."

The other centers of resistance, in Graz, Steuer and Linz, were all crushed. Bauer, Deutsch and many others fled into Czechoslovakia. Wallisch, caught near the frontier, was hanged at Loeben, in a brightly lighted courtyard, while his socialist fellow-prisoners looked on. "Long live freedom!" he shouted. The hangman and his assistants pulled him from the scaffold and clung to his legs until he choked.

Bergmann sat in his chair facing the set, grim, and silent, like an accusing specter. One morning, Eliot ventured to ask him how he had liked a take.

"I loved it," Bergmann told him, savagely. "I loved it. It was unspeakably horrible. It was the maximum of filth. Never in my whole life have I seen anything so idiotic."

"You want to shoot it again, sir?"

"Yes, by all means. Let us shoot it again. Perhaps we can achieve something worse. I doubt it. But let us try."

Eliot grinned nervously, trying to pass this off as a joke.

"So?" Bergmann turned on him suddenly. "You find this amusing? You do not believe me? Very well—let me see you direct this scene yourself."

Eliot looked scared. "I couldn't do that, sir."

"You mean that you refuse to do it? You definitely refuse? Is that what you mean?"

"No, sir. Of course not. But ..."

"You prefer that I ask Dorothy to direct this scene?"

"No ..." Eliot, poor boy, was almost in tears.

"Then obey me!" Bergmann flared at him. "Do what I order!"

All that week, he seemed to be possessed by a devil. He tried to quarrel with everybody, even the loyal Teddy and Roger. We moved to another small set—a room in the Borodanian palace. Harris was present when Bergmann inspected it. I knew there would be trouble.

Bergmann found fault with everything. "In which *stables*," he asked Harris, "did you get these curtains?" Then he discovered that one of the doors wouldn't open.

"Sorry, sir," the carpenter explained, "we didn't have no orders it was to be made practical."

Bergmann snorted frantically. He walked up to the door and gave it a violent kick. We looked on, wondering what was coming. Suddenly, he swung round upon us.

"And there you all stand," he shouted, "grinning at me like evil, stubborn monkeys!"

He stormed out. We avoided each other's eyes. It was ridiculous, of course. But Bergmann's rage was so genuine, and somehow so touching, that nobody wanted to laugh.

An instant later, his tousled head popped in through a window of the set, like an infuriated Punch.

"No!" he cried. "Not monkeys! Donkeys!"

It would have been kindest, perhaps, to shout back at him, to afford him the exquisite relief of a fight. But none of us would do it. Some were sorry for him, some sulky and offended, some embarrassed, some scared. I was a bit scared of him, myself. The others assumed that I could manage him; but they were quite wrong. "You talk to him, Chris," Teddy would tell me. And once he added, with surprising insight, "Talk to him in German. It'll make him feel more at home."

But what was I to say? To have tried to excuse Bergmann's outbursts to himself would merely have made things worse. I knew he was ashamed of them, five minutes later. I only avoided his rage by keeping very close to him. Though he took little notice of me, he needed my presence, as a lonely man needs his dog. There was nothing I could do to help, except to maintain our contact.

I was with him nearly every evening, until he was tired enough to go to bed and lie still. I don't think he slept much. I would have offered to spend the night on the couch in his living room, but I knew he would resent that. I couldn't treat him as an invalid.

One evening, while we were having supper in a restaurant, a man named Patterson came up to our table. He was a journalist, who did a movie gossip column for one of the daily papers, and spent most of his time hunting for news around the studios. He had visited our unit once or twice, to talk to Anita. He was a breezy, stupid, thick-skinned person, whose curiosity knew no inhibitions; in fact, he was very well suited to his job.

"Well, Mr. Bergmann," he began heartily, with the fatal instinct of the very tactless, "what do you think of Austria?"

My heart sank. I tried, weakly, to interrupt and change the subject. But it was already too late. Bergmann stiffened. His eyes flashed. He thrust his head forward across the table, accusingly.

"What do *you* think of Austria, Mr. Patterson?"

The journalist was rather taken aback, as most of them are, when you ask them questions. "Well, as a matter of fact, I ... It's terrible, of course. . . ."

Bergmann gathered himself together, and struck out at him like a snake. "I will tell you what you think. You think nothing. Nothing whatsoever."

Patterson blinked. But he was too stupid to realize he had better drop the subject. "Of course," he said, "I don't pretend to know much about politics, but ..."

"This has nothing to do with politics. This has to do with plain human men and women.

Not with actresses and indiscreet whores. Not with celluloid. Not with self-advertisement. With flesh and with blood. And you do not think about it. You do not care one damn."

Even now, Patterson wasn't really rattled. "After all, Mr. Bergmann," he said defensively, with his silly, teasing, insensitive smile, "you must remember, it isn't our affair. I mean, you can't really expect people in England to care . . ."

Bergmann's fist hit the table, so that the knives and forks rang. He turned scarlet in the face. He shouted, "I expect everybody to care! Everybody who is not a coward, a moron, a piece of dirt! I expect this whole damned island to care! I will tell you something: if they do not care, they will be made to care. The whole lot of you. You will be bombed and slaughtered and conquered. And do you know what I shall do? I shall sit by and smoke my cigar and laugh. And I shall say, 'Yes, it's terrible; and I do not give a damn. Not *one* damn.' "

Patterson, at last, was looking a bit scared.

"Don't get me wrong, Mr. Bergmann," he said, hastily. "I quite agree with you. I'm on your side entirely. Oh, yes . . . We don't think enough of the other fellow, and that's a fact . . . Well, I must be toddling along. Glad to have seen you. We must have a talk, some day. . . . Good night."

We were alone. Bergmann was still fuming. He breathed hard, watching me out of the corner of his eye. I knew that he was waiting for me to make some comment.

And I couldn't. That night, as never before, I felt emotionally exhausted. Bergmann's intense, perpetual demand had drained me, it seemed, of the last drop of response. I no longer knew what I felt—only what I was supposed to feel. My only emotion, as always in such moments, was a weak resentment against both sides; against Bergmann, against Patterson, and against myself. "Why can't they leave me alone?" I resentfully exclaimed. But the "I" that thought this was both Patterson and Bergmann, Englishman and Austrian, islander and Continental. It was divided, and hated its division.

Perhaps I had traveled too much, left my heart in too many places. I knew what I was supposed to feel, what it was fashionable for my generation to feel. We cared about everything: fascism in Germany and Italy, the seizure of Manchuria, Indian nationalism, the Irish question, the workers, the Negroes, the Jews. We had spread our feelings over the whole world; and I knew that mine were spread very thin. I cared —oh, yes, I certainly cared—about the Austrian socialists. But did I care as much as I said I did, tried to imagine I did? No, not nearly as much. I felt angry with Patterson; but he, at least, was honest. What is the use of caring at all, if you aren't prepared to dedicate your life, to die? Well, perhaps it was some use. Very, very little.

Bergmann must have known what I was thinking. After a long silence, he said, kindly and gently, "You are tired, my child. Go to bed."

We parted at the restaurant door. I watched him walking away down the street, his head sunk in thought, until he was lost among the crowd.

I had failed him; I knew it. But I could do no more. It was beyond my strength.

That night, I think, he explored the uttermost depths of his loneliness.

Next morning, Ashmeade came onto the set. I wondered why. He seemed to have no special mission. He nodded to Bergmann, but didn't engage him in conversation. For some time, he stood watching, with a faint secret smile on his lips.

Presently, Bergmann walked off into a corner, to speak to Dorothy. This must have been what Ashmeade was waiting for. He turned to me.

"Oh, Isherwood, can you spare me a minute of your valuable time?"

We strolled away together, toward the other end of the stage.

"You know," Ashmeade told me, in his soft, flattering voice, "Chatsworth's very grateful to you. In fact, we all are."

"Oh, really?" I was cautious, somehow suspecting this opening.

"We quite realize," Ashmeade chose each word, smiling, as if it tasted nice, "that you're in rather a difficult position. I think you've shown a great deal of tact and patience. We appreciate that."

"I'm afraid I don't understand," I said. I knew exactly what he was driving at now. And he knew that I knew. He was enjoying this little game.

"Well, I'm going to be frank with you. This is between ourselves, of course. . . . Chatsworth's getting worried. He simply can't understand Bergmann's attitude."

"How dreadful!" My tone was thoroughly

nasty. Ashmeade gave me one of his poker-face looks.

"Everybody's complaining about him," he continued, his voice becoming confidential. "Anita talked to us yesterday. She wants to be released from the picture. We wouldn't agree to it, of course. But you can't blame her. After all, she's a big star. Bergmann treats her like a bit player.... It isn't only Anita, either. Harris feels the same way. So does Watts. They're prepared to put up with a good deal of temperament from a director. But there's a limit."

I said nothing. I hated having to agree with Ashmeade.

"You two are still great friends, aren't you?" It sounded like a playful accusation.

"Better than ever," I told him, defiantly.

"Well, can't you give us some idea of what's the matter with him? Isn't he happy here? What's he got against us?"

"Nothing ... It's hard to explain.... You know he's been worried about his family. . . ."

"Oh, yes, this business in Austria ... But that's all over now, isn't it?"

"On the contrary. It's probably just beginning."

"But I mean, the fighting has stopped. And his family's safe. What more does he want?"

"Look here, Ashmeade," I said. "It's no use our talking about this. You couldn't possibly understand. . . . You want the picture finished. I see that. Just be patient, a little. He'll come round."

"I hope you're right," Ashmeade gave me a playfully wry smile. "It's costing the studio a lot of money."

"He'll come round," I repeated, confidently. "You'll see. I'm sure it's going to be all right."

But I wasn't sure. I wasn't even hopeful. And Ashmeade knew it.

I don't know exactly how the whole thing started. Two days later, I overheard Joyce saying something to Clark about Eddie Kennedy. It would have made no impression on me if they hadn't stopped talking and looked guilty and slightly gleeful as I came up.

Several times that morning, I heard Kennedy's name. Fred Murray said it. Roger was mentioning it in a conversation with Timmy. Prince Rudolf was murmuring it to Count Rosanoff, as they waited to rehearse a scene. They glanced toward Bergmann, and their faces betrayed a discreet satisfaction.

Then, while we were in the sound booth together, Roger said to me, "I suppose you've heard? Eddie Kennedy looked at our rushes this morning."

For the moment, I didn't understand what he meant.

"That's funny," I said. "I was in the projection room myself. I didn't see him."

Roger smiled. "Of course you didn't. He saw them later. After you and Bergmann had gone."

"I wonder why?"

Roger gave me a glance, as though he thought I might be acting innocent. "There's only one explanation, Chris. Figure it out for yourself."

"You mean—they're going to put him on this picture?"

"I don't see what else it can mean."

"Gosh ..."

"Do you think Bergmann knows?" Roger asked.

I shook my head. "He'd have told me."

"For Christ's sake, Chris, don't tell him I told you this."

"Do you suppose I want to talk about it?"

"I'm sorry for Bergmann," said Roger, thoughtfully. "He's had bad luck here. I don't care if he does sound off sometimes. He's a decent old bird. ... I wish this didn't have to happen. Besides, Eddie could no more direct this picture than a drunken cow."

My one cowardly idea was: Bergmann has got to hear this from somebody else, and not when I'm around. At lunchtime, I tried to sneak away; but he was watching for me. "Come," he said, "we shall eat at the hotel." This was exactly what I had feared.

Sure enough, Kennedy was there, sitting with Ashmeade. They were deep in conversation. Kennedy seemed to be outlining some plan. He had arranged his knife, fork and spoon in a square, and was demonstrating something with the pepper-pot. Neither of them took any notice of us; but, as we passed, Ashmeade looked at Kennedy and laughed an intimate, flattering laugh. Several of the other Bulldog directors and executives regarded us curiously. I could feel their eyes following our backs.

During the meal, Bergmann was thoughtful and moody. We scarcely spoke. I had to force myself to eat. I felt as if I were going to vomit. Should I tell him? No, I couldn't. I waited for something to happen.

We had nearly finished when Patterson, the journalist, came in.

He greeted everybody, stopping at each

group for a joke and a word or two; but I knew instinctively that he was making for our table. His face was beaming, it seemed to me, with the malice of the stupid man who thinks he is going to score a point.

"Well, well, Mr. Bergmann," he began, sitting down without being invited. "What's all this I hear? Is it really true?"

"Is what true?" Bergmann looked at him with distaste.

"About the picture. You're really dropping it?"

"Dropping?"

"Retiring. Giving it up."

For a moment, it seemed that Bergmann still didn't understand him. Then he jerked out, "Who told you this?"

"Oh, well, you know," Patterson looked maliciously coy, "these things get about." He watched Bergmann's face inquisitively. Then he turned to me, with a most unconvincing display of anxiety. "I say, I hope I haven't put my foot in it?"

"I never pay much attention to studio gossip," I said incautiously, in the agony of my embarrassment.

Bergmann turned on me, quite savagely. "You heard this, too?"

138

"There must be some mistake, of course," Patterson was now openly malicious, "if *you* know nothing about it, Mr. Bergmann. . . . It's a funny thing, though. I got this from pretty high up. It certainly sounded authentic. Eddie Kennedy was mentioned. . . ."

"Oh, if that's all it was . . ." (I was desperately trying to give Bergmann a chance of pretending he knew this already.) "It's quite easily explained. Just because he saw our rushes this morning . . . You know how these things are misrepresented. . . ."

But Bergmann was beyond all diplomacy.

"Kennedy saw the rushes? And I knew nothing about it! Nothing! I wasn't told!" He swung round upon me, again. "You knew this all the time? You were in this conspiracy against me?"

"I—I didn't think it was important. . . ."

"Not important! Oh, no! If I am betrayed and tricked and lied to, it is not in the least important! If my only friend joins the enemy, it is not important!" Suddenly, he turned back to Patterson. "Who told you this?"

"Well, really, Mr. Bergmann—I'm not at liberty to say."

"Of course you are not at liberty to say! These people are your paymasters! Very good: I will tell you who it was. Ashmeade!"

Patterson tried to look inscrutable. He didn't succeed.

"It was Ashmeade!" cried Bergmann, triumphantly. "I knew it!" He spoke so loud that the people at the next table stared at us. "I shall confront him immediately with this impudent lie!"

He jumped to his feet.

"Friedrich!" I grabbed his arm. "Wait. Not now."

My tone must have been commanding in its desperation, for Bergmann hesitated.

"We'll talk to him at the studio," I continued. "It'll be better. Let's think this over first."

Bergmann nodded and sat down again.

"Very well, we shall deal with him later," he agreed, breathing hard. "First, we must see his master. At once. After lunch."

"All right." My one idea was to pacify him. "After lunch."

"I'm afraid I've been the bearer of evil tidings," said Patterson, with a smirk. At that moment, I really hated him.

"Look here," I said, "you aren't going to print any of this?"

"Well . . ." Patterson became cagey, at once. "I'll have to get it confirmed, naturally. . . . If

Mr. Bergmann would care to make a statement. . . ."

"He wouldn't," I interrupted, firmly.

"I shall make a statement," said Bergmann. "Undoubtedly I shall make a statement. This is nothing secret. Let the whole world know of this betrayal. I shall write to every newspaper. I shall reveal how a foreign director, a guest in this country, is betrayed. I regard this as a clear stab in the back. It is discrimination. It is persecution. I shall bring an action for damages."

"I'm quite sure," I told Patterson, "that everything will be explained satisfactorily. You'll know by this evening."

Bergmann merely snorted.

"Well," said Patterson, with his teasing smile, "I hope so, I'm sure. . . . Good-bye, Mr. Bergmann." He left us, delightedly. We saw him go straight over to Ashmeade's table.

"That dirty spy," Bergman hissed. "Now he makes his report."

When we went out of the dining room, a few minutes later, Patterson, Ashmeade and Kennedy were still sitting together. I took Bergmann's arm, resolved, if necessary, to prevent him from speaking to them by force. But he contented himself with saying, very loudly, as we passed, "Judas Iscariot is in council with the High Priests."

Neither Ashmeade nor Patterson looked at us, but Kennedy grinned pleasantly, and called, "Hi, Bergmann. How's everything?"

Bergmann didn't answer.

I had hoped that the taxi ride would have given him time to cool down. But it didn't. As soon as we were back at our office in the studio, he told Dorothy, "Call Mr. Chatsworth, and say I demand to see him immediately."

Dorothy picked up the telephone. She was informed that Chatsworth was still out at lunch. Bergmann grunted dangerously.

Eliot came in.

"All ready to rehearse the restaurant scene, sir."

Bergmann glared at him. "There will be no shooting today."

"No shooting?" Eliot echoed, stupidly.

"You heard what I said."

"But, Mr. Bergmann, we're behind schedule already, and . . ."

"There will be no shooting today!" Bergmann shouted at him. "Is that clear?"

Eliot crumpled. "What time shall I make the call for tomorrow?" he ventured to ask, at length.

"I don't know and I don't care!"

I signaled to Eliot with my eyes to leave us alone. He went out, with a deep sigh.

"Call Chatsworth again," Bergmann ordered.

But Chatsworth was still out. Half an hour later he had returned and gone immediately into conference. An hour later, he was still busy.

"Very well," said Bergmann. "We also can play at this game of rat and mouse. Come, we go home. I shall not return here. Chatsworth shall come to see me, and I shall be too busy. Tell him that."

He struggled furiously into his overcoat. The telephone rang.

"Mr. Chatsworth will see you now," Dorothy reported.

I gasped with relief. Bergmann scowled. He seemed disappointed.

"Come," he said to me.

In Chatsworth's outer office, as ill-luck would have it, there was another delay. This gave Bergmann's temper time to reach boiling point again. He began to mutter to himself. At the end of five minutes, he said, "Enough of this farce. Come. We go."

"Couldn't you . . ." I appealed desperately to

the girl at the desk, "couldn't you tell him it's
urgent?"

The girl looked embarrassed. "Mr. Chatsworth particularly told me not to disturb him.
He's on the line to Paris," she said.

"Enough!" cried Bergmann. "We go!"

"Friedrich! Please wait another minute!"

"You desert me? Splendid! I go alone."

"Oh, very well . . ." I rose unwillingly to my
feet.

The inner door opened. It was Ashmeade,
grinning all over his face. "Won't you come in,
please?" he said.

Bergmann didn't even glance at him. With a
fearful snort, like a bull entering the ring, he
strode into the room, head lowered. Chatsworth was lolling at his desk, cigar in hand, He
flourished it toward the chairs.

"Take a pew, gentlemen!"

But Bergmann didn't sit down. "First," he
nearly shouted, "I demand absolutely that this
Fouché, this spy, shall leave the room!"

Ashmeade kept on smiling, but I could see
that he was disconcerted. Chatsworth looked
squarely at Bergmann from behind his thick
spectacles.

"Don't be silly," he said, good-humoredly.
"Nobody's going to leave any rooms. If you've

got something to say, say it. This is as much Sandy's business as mine."

Bergmann growled. "So you protect him?"

"Certainly," Chatsworth was quite unruffled. "I protect all my subordinates. Until they're sacked. And I do the sacking."

"You will not sack me!" Bergmann yelled. "I do not give you that pleasure. I resign!"

"You do, eh? Well, my directors are always resigning. All except the lousy ones, worse luck."

"Such as Mr. Kennedy, for example?"

"Eddie? Oh, he walks out on every picture. He's great."

"You make fun of me!"

"Sorry, old boy. You're pretty funny yourself, you know."

Bergmann was so angry he couldn't answer. He turned on his heel and made for the door. I stood undecided, watching him.

"Listen," said Chatsworth, with such authority that Bergmann stopped.

"I shall not listen. Not to your insults."

"Nobody's going to insult you. Sit down."

To my amazement, Bergmann did so. My opinion of Chatsworth was rising every moment.

"Listen to me . . ." Chatsworth punctured his

145

sentences with puffs at his cigar. "You walk off the picture. You break your contract. All right. You know what you're doing, I suppose. That's your affair, and the Legal Department's. But meanwhile, somebody has to shoot this God-damned movie...."

"I am not interested!" Bergmann interrupted. "The picture means nothing to me any more. This is a case of abstract justice...."

"Somebody," Chatsworth continued, imperturbably, "has to shoot this picture. And I have to see that it's shot...."

"My work is spied upon. Behind my back, the rushes are shown to this ignorant cretin...."

"Let's get this straight," said Chatsworth. "Eddie was shown the rushes by Sandy, quite unofficially, because Sandy was worried about the way the picture was going. He wanted an outside opinion. I knew nothing about it. As a matter of fact, Sandy was taking a risk. He was breaking a studio rule. I might have been very angry with him. But, under the circumstances, I think he did perfectly right.... I know you've been under the weather lately. I know your wife and daughter were in Vienna during this little spot of bother, and I'm damn sorry. That's why I've kept quiet as long as I have. But I can't throw away the studio's money because of your private sorrows, or mine, or anybody else's. . . ."

"And so you invite this analphabet to take my place?"

"I hadn't got as far as thinking of anybody taking your place. I didn't know you were going to walk out on us."

"And now you set this Kennedy to work, who will carefully annihilate every fragment Isherwood and I have built up, so lovingly, all these months . . ."

"A lot of it's damn good, I admit. . . . But what am I to do? You've left us in the lurch."

(Oh, gosh, I thought, he's smart!)

"Everything destroyed. Obliterated. Reduced to utter nonsense. Terrible. Nothing to do."

"What do you care? You're not interested in the picture."

Bergmann's eyes flashed. "Who says I am not?"

"You did."

"I said nothing of the kind. I said I am not interested in the picture which your Kennedy will make."

"You said you weren't interested. . . . Didn't he, Sandy?"

"It is a lie!" Bergmann glared at Ashmeade. "I could never say such a thing! How could I not be interested? For this picture, I have given everything—all my time, all my thought, all my care, all my strength, since months. Who dares to say I am not interested?"

"Atta boy!" Chatsworth began to laugh very heartily. Getting to his feet, he came around the desk and slapped Bergmann on the shoulder. "That's the spirit! Of course you're interested! I always knew you were. If anybody says you're not, I'll help you beat the hell out of him." He paused, as if struck by a sudden idea. "And now, I'll tell you what: you and I and Isherwood are going down to look at those rushes together. And we won't take Sandy along, either. That'll be his punishment, the dirty dog."

By this time, Chatsworth had walked Bergmann right over to the door. Bergmann looked somewhat dazed. He didn't resist at all. Chatsworth held the door open for us. As I went out, I saw him wink at Ashmeade over his shoulder.

Down in the projection room, they were waiting for us. We sat through the day's rushes. Then Chatsworth said, quite casually, "Suppose we look at everything you've shot these last two weeks?"

My suspicions turned to certainty. I whispered to Lawrence Dwight, "When did Chatsworth arrange for this stuff to be shown?"

"Early this morning," said Lawrence. "Why?"

"Oh, nothing." I smiled to myself in the darkness. So that was that.

When it was all over, and the lights went up, Chatsworth asked, "Well, how does it look?"

"It's terrible," said Bergmann gloomily. "Definitely horrible."

"Oh, now I wouldn't go so far as that," Chatsworth puffed blandly at his cigar. "That scene of Anita's is damn good."

"You are wrong," Bergmann brightened at once. "It is terrible."

"I like your camera angles."

"I hate them. It is so poor, so dull. It is without mood. It is just a lousy newsreel."

"I don't see what you could have done better."

"You do not see," said Bergmann, actually smiling. "But I see. I see clearly. The approach is wrong. My eyes are opened. I have been fumbling in the dark, like an old idiot."

"You think you can cure it?"

"Beginning tomorrow," said Bergmann, with decision, "I reshoot everything. I work night and day. It is perfectly clear to me. We shall keep our schedule. We shall make you a great picture."

"Of course you will!" Chatsworth put his arm around Bergmann's neck. "But you'll have to sell me your new ideas first. . . . Look here, let's have dinner together this evening, the three of us? Then we'll get down to brass tacks."

If I had imagined we kept long hours before, I was wrong. The days which followed were unlike anything else I have ever known. I lost all sense of space and time, I was so tired. Everybody was tired, and yet we worked better than ever before. Even the actors didn't sulk.

Bergmann inspired us all. His absolute certainty swept us along like a torrent. There were hardly any retakes. The necessary script alterations seemed to write themselves. Bergmann knew exactly what he wanted. We took everything in our stride.

Incredibly soon, the last days of shooting arrived. One night (perhaps it was the last night of all; I don't remember) we worked very late, on the big opening scene at the Prater. Bergmann, that evening, was unforgettable. Very haggard, with blazing dark eyes in the furrowed mask of his face, he maneuvered the great crowd this way and that, molded it, reduced it to a single organism, in which every individual had a part. We were exhausted, but we were all laughing. It was like a party, and Bergmann was our host.

When the last take was finished, he came solemnly up to Anita, in front of everybody, and kissed her hand. "Thank you, my darling," he said. "You were great."

Anita loved it. Her eyes filled with tears.

"Friedrich, I'm sorry I was naughty sometimes. I shall never have an experience like this again. I think you're the most wonderful man in the world."

"Well," said Lawrence Dwight, addressing his artificial leg, "now we've seen everything, haven't we, Stump?"

Arthur Cromwell had a flat in Chelsea. Wouldn't we all go round there for a nightcap? Anita said yes. So of course Bergmann and I had to accept. Eliot and Lawrence and Harris joined us. And Bergmann insisted on bringing Dorothy, Teddy and Roger. Then, just as we were starting, Ashmeade appeared.

I was afraid there would be a row—but no. I saw Bergmann stiffen a little. Then Ashmeade took him aside and said something, smiling his subtly flattering smile.

"You go with the others," Bergmann told me. "Ashmeade will drive me in his car. He wants to talk to me."

I don't know what they said to each other; but when we all arrived at Cromwell's flat, it was obvious that a reconciliation had taken place. Bergmann was sparkling, and Ashmeade's smile had become intimate. After a few minutes, I heard him call Bergmann "Friedrich." And, more marvelous still, Bergmann publicly addressed him as "Umbrella."

At the party which followed, Bergmann was terrific. He clowned, he told stories, he sang songs, he imitated German actors, he showed Anita how to dance the *Schuhplattler*. His eyes shone with that last reserve of energy which one puts out in moments of extreme exhaustion, with the aid of a few drinks. And I felt so happy in his success. The way you feel when your father is a success with your friends.

It must have been close on four o'clock when we said good night. Eliot offered us a ride in his car. Bergmann said he preferred to walk.

"I'm coming with you," I told him. I knew that I wouldn't be able to sleep. I was wound up like a watch. In Knightsbridge, I could probably find a taxi to take me home.

It was that hour of the night when the street lamps seem to shine with an unnatural, remote brilliance, like planets on which there is no life. The King's Road was wet-black, and deserted as the moon. It did not belong to the King, or to any human being. The little houses had shut their doors against all strangers and were still, waiting for dawn, bad news and the milk. There was nobody about. Not even a policeman. Not even a cat.

It was that hour of the night at which man's ego almost sleeps. The sense of identity, of possession, of name and address and telephone number grows very faint. It was the hour at which man shivers, pulls up his coat collar, and thinks, "I am a traveler. I have no home."

A traveler, a wanderer. I was aware of Bergmann, my fellow-traveler, pacing beside me: a separate, secret consciousness, locked away within itself, distant as Betelgeuse, yet for a short while, sharing my wanderings. Head thrust forward, hat perched on the thick bush of hair, muffler huddled around the throat under the gray stubble, hands clasped behind the back. Like me, he had his journey to go.

What was he thinking about? *Prater Violet*, his wife, his daughter, myself, Hitler, a poem he would write, his boyhood, or tomorrow

153

morning? How did it feel to be inside that stocky body, to look out of those dark, ancient eyes? How did it feel to be Friedrich Bergmann?

There is one question which we seldom ask each other directly: it is too brutal. And yet it is the only question worth asking our fellow-travelers. What makes you go on living? Why don't you kill yourself? Why is all this bearable? What makes you bear it?

Could I answer that question about myself? No. Yes. Perhaps ... I supposed, vaguely, that it was a kind of balance, a complex of tensions. You did whatever was next on the list. A meal to be eaten. Chapter eleven to be written. The telephone rings. You go off somewhere in a taxi. There is one's job. There are amusements. There are people. There are books. There are things to be bought in shops. There is always something new. There has to be. Otherwise, the balance would be upset, the tension would break.

It seemed to me that I had always done whatever people recommended. You were born; it was like entering a restaurant. The waiter came forward with a lot of suggestions. You said, "What do you advise?" And you ate it, and supposed you liked it, because it was expensive, or out of season, or had been a favorite of King Edward the Seventh. The waiter had recommended teddy bears, football, cigarettes, motor bikes, whisky, Bach, poker, the culture of Classical Greece. Above all, he had recommended Love: a very strange dish.

Love. At the very word, the taste, the smell of it, something inside me began to throb. Ah yes, Love . . . Love, at the moment, was J.

Love had been J. for the last month—ever since we met at that party. Ever since the letter which had arrived next morning, opening the way to the unhoped-for, the unthinkable, the after-all-quite-thinkable and, as it now seemed, absolutely inevitable success of which my friends were mildly envious. Next week, or as soon as my work for Bulldog was finished, we should go away together. To the South of France, perhaps. And it would be wonderful. We would swim. We would lie in the sun. We would take photographs. We would sit in the café. We would hold hands, at night, looking out over the sea from the balcony of our room. I would be so grateful, so flattered, and I would be damned careful not to show it. I would be anxious. I would be jealous. I would unpack my box of tricks, and exhibit them, once again.

And, in the end (the end you never thought about), I would get sick of the tricks, or J. would get sick of them. And very politely, tenderly, nostalgically, flatteringly, we would part. We would part, agreeing to be the greatest friends always. We would part, immune, in future, from that particular toxin, that special twinge of jealous desire, when one of us met the other, with somebody else, at another party.

I was glad I had never told Bergmann about J. He would have taken possession of that, as he did of everything else. But it was still mine, and it would always be. Even when J. and I were only trophies, hung up in the museums of each other's vanity.

After J., there would be K. and L. and M., right down the alphabet. It's no use being sentimentally cynical about this, or cynically sentimental. Because J. isn't really what I want. J. has only the value of being now. J. will pass, the need will remain. The need to get back into the dark, into the bed, into the warm naked embrace, where J. is no more J. than K., L., or M. Where there is nothing but the nearness, and the painful hopelessness of clasping the naked body in your arms. The pain of hunger beneath everything. And the end of all love-making, the dreamless sleep after the orgasm, which is like death.

Death, the desired, the feared. The longed-for sleep. The terror of the coming of sleep. Death. War. The vast sleeping city, doomed for the bombs. The roar of oncoming engines. The gunfire. The screams. The houses shattered. Death universal. My own death. Death of the seen and known and tasted and tangible world. Death with its army of fears. Not the acknowledged fears, the fears that are advertised. More dreadful than those: the private fears of childhood. Fear of the height of the high-dive, fear of the farmer's dog and the vicar's pony, fear of cupboards, fear of the dark passage, fear of splitting your fingernail with a chisel. And behind them, most unspeakably terrible of all, the arch-fear: the fear of being afraid.

It can never be escaped—never, never. Not if you run away to the ends of the earth (we had turned into Sloane Street), not if you yell for Mummy, or keep a stiff upper lip, or take to drink or to dope. That fear sits throned in my heart. I carry it about with me, always.

But if it is mine, if it is really within me . . . Then . . . Why, then . . . And, at this moment, but how infinitely faint, how distant, like the high far glimpse of a goat track through the mountains between clouds, I see something else: the way that leads to safety. To where there is no fear, no loneliness, no need of J., K., L., or M. For a second, I glimpse it. For an instant, it is even quite clear. Then the clouds shut down, and a breath off the glacier, icy with the inhuman coldness of the peaks, touches my cheek. "No," I think, "I could never do it. Rather the fear I know, the loneliness I know . . . For to take that other way would mean that I should lose myself. I should no longer be a person. I should no longer be Christopher Isherwood. No, no. That's more terrible than the bombs. More terrible than having no lover. That I can never face."

Perhaps I might have turned to Bergmann and asked, "Who are you? Who am I? What are we doing here?" But actors cannot ask such questions during the performance. We had written each other's parts, Christopher's Friedrich, Friedrich's Christopher, and we had to go on playing them, as long as we were together. The dialogue was crude, the costumes and make-up were more absurd, more of a caricature, than anything in *Prater Violet*: Mother's Boy, the comic Foreigner with the funny accent. Well, that didn't matter. (We had reached Bergmann's door, now.) For, beneath our disguises, and despite all the kind-unkind things we might ever say or think about each other, we knew. Beneath outer consciousness, two other beings, anonymous, impersonal, without labels, had met and recognized each other, and had clasped hands. He was my father. I was his son. And I loved him very much.

Bergmann held out his hand.

"Good night, my child," he said.

He went into the house.

I never saw *Prater Violet*, after all.

It was shown in London, with a great deal of publicity, and got very good notices. ("When we saw your name on the screen," my mother wrote, "we both felt *very* proud, and applauded loudly. Richard kept saying, 'Isn't that *just* like Christopher?' But, I must say, Anita Hayden is hardly one's idea of an *innocent young girl!* She has a charming voice . . .") It went to New York, and the Americans liked it, unusually well for a British picture. It was even shown in Vienna.

Several months later, I got a letter from Lawrence Dwight, who was on holiday in Paris:

A girl I know here came to me in great indignation the other day. She's an earnest Red, and admires the political consciousness of the French workers; but, alas, it seems that the ones in our neighborhood are all going to see *La Violette du Prater*, a horrible British picture which, besides being an insult to the intelligence of a five-year-old child, is definitely counter-revolutionary and ought to be banned. Meanwhile, in the cinema round the corner, a wonderful Russian masterpiece is playing to empty seats.

Incidentally, I've seen the Russian film, myself. It is the usual sex triangle between a girl with thick legs, a boy, and a tractor. As a matter of fact, it's technically superior to anything Bulldog could produce in a hundred years. But you can't expect the poor fools to know that . . .

As for Bergmann, *Prater Violet* got him the offer of a job in Hollywood. He went out there with his family, early in 1935.